It took only a few seconds to kill Frances Rassell with a thin wire pulled tightly around her neck. Frances's killer bent over the body and opened the handbag still hanging from her wrist. Except for a nearly empty wallet, a handkerchief, and a comb, there was nothing to be found. It took another second for a compact wire cutter to snip the chain that held the gate closed.

Frances's body rolled easily down the ramp to the bottom of the hole. The killer refastened the gate enough to hold it shut, then looked around quickly. The streets harbored no strollers in the snow, which had started to fall again more heavily. The security guard on duty at the construction site was not in view.

Even before the killer departed, a light blanket of white had begun to cover Frances's sensible dark coat and her gray knitted hat. Soon she was just another mound of debris at the bottom of the pit.

IT'S HER FUNERAL

Joyce Christmas

FAWCETT GOLD MEDAL • NEW YORK

A Fawcett Gold Medal Book
Published by Ballantine Books
Copyright © 1992 by Joyce Christmas

All rights reserved under International and Pan-American Copyright Conventions. Published in the United States by Ballantine Books, a division of Random House, Inc., New York, and simultaneously in Canada by Random House of Canada Limited, Toronto.

Library of Congress Catalog Card Number: 92-90150

ISBN 0-449-14702-9

Manufactured in the United States of America

First Edition: August 1992

For Lenny Fogel.
Thanks

Chapter 1

Frances Rassell waited in the freezing night beside the wooden fencing that had been erected to keep neighborhood children from tumbling into the construction site. She peered down the street, but all she saw was the headlights of a car proceeding slowly. A neighborhood resident looking for a rare parking space still open at eight at night.

Meeting outside in the cold hadn't been her idea. She had a perfectly good warm house two blocks away, but no. It had to be here, too many eyes watching who was coming and going at her place. That's what a neighborhood was supposed to be: people watching out for one another. That's what she had always tried to do, even if some people didn't understand that.

The construction site was still only a big hole in the ground with a steep earthen ramp to allow the trucks to go down and bring up debris and earth where now-demolished buildings had stood for most of the twentieth century: once proud brownstones, a few stores, abandoned warehouses. Years ago, the factory where her husband worked had stood at the far end of the site, but he had died by the time it was torn down and the land turned into a parking lot.

The dynamiting was scheduled to start soon in earnest. She had already heard a few blasts after the warning whistles and had felt the ground shake while her pretty Hummel figurines jumped in their glass-fronted cabinet. Before long, more trucks would rumble into the neighborhood, and tall cranes would appear to lift up the steel girders. In a year or so, a massive glass tower would stand above the low, grimy buildings of the neighborhood. Frances and her neighbors would live in its shadow. She had seen the model, and it had looked really nice.

It was colder than she had thought, although the faint sifting of snow had stopped. Her old bones felt the cold more than they used to. She pulled her gray knitted cap down around her ears and stuffed her hands into her coat pockets. Her black Leatherette handbag dangled by its strap over her wrist.

Frances felt responsible for the neighborhood. All the others were out for themselves, and some of them resented her. She knew it, but it wasn't stopping her from doing what was right.

Her daughter, Alice, out on Long Island with that husband of hers and the kids, had no sympathy. "You like poking your nose into everybody's business, Ma," she'd say when she bothered to call. And then, inevitably, "How much do you think our old house is going to be worth with this building going up?" Alice was too greedy for her own good, and she had it easy. She didn't have to listen to the noisy factions for and against the new building, people who didn't want to compromise, with bad feelings all around and new troubles every day. Frances could name the troublemakers if she wanted to. She could tell some tales that would change people's minds about a lot of things that were going on. And she'd speak up if she had to. She was going to speak up tonight and get some answers, or she'd know the reason why.

It was getting past the time for her appointment. She would wait a few more minutes and then go home.

Toward the west, Frances could see a bit of Manhattan—the top of the Empire State Building with red, white, and blue lights, the thin spire of the Chrysler Building. Things were different over there. She never imagined that her part of Queens would begin to mimic the big city on the other side of the East River, with office towers and these fancy new condominiums and shiny banks and shops. She never imagined she'd be a part of it. Once the building was finished, the neighborhood could really hold its head up.

She saw a figure coming along the sidewalk toward her, past the lighted windows of the three-story houses that were now mostly apartments, one to a floor and full of newcomers. She waved, and the person trudging along, bundled up against the cold, waved back. Frances was relieved. It wasn't some dangerous stranger. Arcadia used to be a really safe neighborhood in the sixty-odd years she'd lived here, but it wasn't the same now. All these new people moving in— artists and musicians and she didn't know what. Foreigners, too. Black people and those Hispanics and Koreans, even Indians. Then there were the drug addicts getting off the subway to rob you and the cars from New Jersey cruising by, and you didn't want to ask what *they* were looking for.

The vandalism that had started recently troubled her. It had begun suddenly, almost as though it had been planned. The garbage dumped in front of houses, dirty words spray-painted on doors. Motorcycles roaring up and down the streets, phones ringing in the middle of the night, but no one was there. Some of her neighbors were talking more about selling out quickly for as much as they could get. She had a pretty good idea who was behind it, but she didn't have proof. If it was somebody's idea of protesting against the construction, they were too late. The building was going to happen; nobody was going to stop the developers. They had all the zoning and permits they needed.

As soon as the person she was meeting reached her side, Frances said, "I know what's going on, and I'm not going to keep quiet. It's a disgrace. Don't try to stop me." She tried to sound firm and important. She was, after all, the chairperson of the Arcadia Neighborhood Action Committee.

"You're mistaken. I don't know what you think you know, but you're wrong. Trust me."

"You're a fine one to talk," Frances said. "I told you, I have proof, and certain parties are going to find it very interesting." She hugged her handbag as though to protect its contents.

"Do you want money?"

"No," Frances said grimly. "I want to know what you're going to do about it."

It took only a few seconds to kill Frances Rassell with a thin wire pulled tightly around her neck. Frances's killer bent over the body and opened the handbag still hanging from the woman's wrist. Except for a nearly empty wallet, a handkerchief, and a comb, there was nothing to be found. It took another second for a compact wire cutter to snip the chain that held the gate closed.

Frances's body rolled easily down the ramp to the bottom of the hole. The killer refastened the gate enough to hold it shut, then looked around quickly. The streets harbored no strollers in the snow, which had started to fall again, more heavily. The security guard on duty at the construction site was not in view.

Even before the killer departed, a light blanket of white had begun to cover Frances's sensible dark coat and her gray knitted hat. Soon she was just another mound of debris at the bottom of the pit.

Self-righteous indignation and a taste for sharing everything one knew could be distinctly hazardous to one's health.

Chapter 2

"*Margaret, darlin',* how's the weather up there?"

Lady Margaret Priam shifted the phone from one ear to the other and looked out the wide window of her East Side Manhattan high-rise apartment. The sky was still heavy with clouds, but the intermittent snow that had been falling for the past couple of days had ceased for the moment.

"Cold, dreary, damp, and miserable. February in New York, Carolyn Sue," Margaret said. "Where are you?" She could hear a faint crackle on the line.

"Ocho Rios," Carolyn Sue said. "Ben and I like to get away to the Caribbean 'round this time of year, but Mustique is jes' too highfalutin nowadays. You've got your Princess Margaret, and that Mick Jagger . . ." Carolyn Sue seemed to have acquired a remarkable combination of Texas drawl and a West Indian accent. "Not much to interest me in Dallas now, so here we are in Jamaica."

Carolyn Sue Dennis, formerly Princess Castrocani of Rome and now Mrs. Benton Hoopes of Dallas, was significantly rich, so even in tight economic times she could do pretty much what she wanted. If February meant an expensive resort in the Jamaican sun, so be it.

"Set that down there, honey," Carolyn Sue said to some unknown person on her end of the line. "We have a real darlin' maid," she said to Margaret. "They sure do treat you real fine here. Makes me forget all my troubles."

"You don't have troubles," Margaret said cautiously, "do you?" Margaret herself had her share of little troubles. It wasn't all that easy to live well in New York as a titled expatriate English lady in her midthirties with only her modest capital to live on and no immediate prospect of a job for which she was qualified. Lady Margaret was popular with New York society people, to be sure, but she was unwilling to be merely the attractive dinner partner of some recently divorced, out-of-work stockbroker at a gala banquet or a decorative title at the glamorous charity events that continued to exist.

Her gentleman friend, Sam De Vere of the New York police, had only so much time he could spare for her from the monumental struggle to stem the tide of crime. Thus she was left with many idle hours, which couldn't be filled with endless window-shopping, improving books, or even afternoon soap operas. In desperation, she had agreed to be on a committee for a socially acceptable charity group. Good works were often the last resort of the unskilled upper classes.

"Other people have troubles, Carolyn Sue," Margaret said firmly. "Not you."

"Why, Margaret, these times are loaded down with troubles for me. You must have been readin' the papers."

Margaret still couldn't grasp the nature of the troubles that dared to plague Carolyn Sue: the world political situation, the state of the stock market, the lack of really good haute couture coming out of Paris. She hoped Carolyn Sue wasn't getting around to a problem with her son, Prince Paul Castrocani, who was a dear boy and good friend, albeit a decade younger than Margaret. He had been a casualty of cutbacks at United National Bank & Trust, where he had worked ineffectively for a few years learning the New York banking business. De Vere, who shared Paul's Chelsea apartment on an amicable, seldom overlapping basis, had told her that Paul had gone off somewhere to sulk about being unemployed.

"It's not Paul, is it?" Margaret asked.

"Lord, no, Paul's right here with Ben and me, sunning himself and playing in the sea with some real nice girls he's met. He needed a vacation, so Ben asked him to fly down. I'm right pleased that he and his stepdaddy get on so well."

So Paul was all right. In any case, his most serious business was his quest for a rich and beautiful wife, something his father, Prince Aldo, had excelled at, having snared Carolyn Sue briefly three decades ago as she was spending her own daddy's money in Rome.

"What I'm talkin' about is this bitty problem I got up there in New York," Carolyn Sue said. "I thought you might be able to help me out."

Margaret decided quickly that she would be willing to advance upon Cartier or Tiffany's in high dudgeon to demand satisfaction in the matter of a flawed diamond in an expensive piece of jewelry. Anything more complicated, however, was more than she'd care to involve herself in.

"I have this little business matter that's run into a difficulty," Carolyn Sue said. "You know about my real estate development?"

Margaret instantly began to formulate a polite refusal that would not offend Carolyn Sue, whose business affairs were complicated and far-flung and whose holdings and investments were legendary. Real estate was beyond Margaret's scope of competence.

"Perhaps Paul would be better suited to attend to business matters," Margaret said, "assuming he could detach himself from the coral reefs and rum punches."

"I don't think he's right for this," Carolyn Sue said. "It's about this murder."

Margaret sighed. She'd encountered a couple of murders in the past and had sworn off them.

"Really, I couldn't, Carolyn Sue. I promised De Vere that I would not become involved in murder ever again."

"Why, honey, even Sam De Vere couldn't complain about this," Carolyn Sue said. "None of those awful bodies lying around. The body's been taken away, and the police are investigating. This is more like damage control. My old daddy would turn over in that god-awful mausoleum he insisted on building if he thought my reputation was bein' tarnished.''

Margaret seemed to recall that Carolyn Sue's father was often referred to as something of a frontier bandit, but perhaps his middle-aged, jet-setting daughter's reputation was important to him even beyond the grave.

''What is it you want of me?'' Margaret had no choice but to listen.

''It's about this building of mine. In Queens.''

''I know where Queens is, but I haven't heard about your building.''

''It's a bit complicated. One of my companies bought up this messy ol' piece of land and tore down a few houses that were older than my great-granddaddy. Some folks in the neighborhood didn't like the idea, and they started a bit of trouble, protesting and rallying and I don't know what all when we began digging. Mind you, some folks over there liked the idea right from the start. A high-class beauty parlor and real nice restaurants. Office space and apartments. Why, we're even plannin' a multiplex. *Seven* screens.''

''What exactly do you want of me?'' Seven movie screens sounded like wretched excess.

''An old lady who was one of the community leaders went and got herself killed at the construction site. They started saying one o' my people killed her to shut her up, and they're tryin' to get the media all bothered about us wicked, unfeeling multimillionaires who like to step on the little people. Of course, I had nothing to do with her dyin'.''

''I believe you, but I still don't know what I can do,'' Margaret said. She might have read a brief news story about a death and a neighborhood protest, but both things were common enough in New York. Taking a whack at the unfeeling rich was almost as compelling a pastime as recounting the sexual peccadilloes of elected officials and bemoaning the decline of the quality of life in all five boroughs.

''There's going to be a neighborhood meeting tomorrow night,'' Carolyn Sue said. ''I was thinkin' if you went over there as my representative, you could help smooth things over. My board of directors thinks I should jes' keep out of it, but I can't. The building is going to make life better, help the folks who live there, and raise property values. But those people just don't see it. So I decided to offer them these— what do you call 'em?—amenities. I've been holdin' on to a little piece of land that I'll give them for a park—a real financial sacrifice for me, I don't mind saying. And I'll give them space in the new building for the golden agers to meet. They like to play bingo up there, don't they? That would make everybody happy.''

Margaret didn't think that the upheaval of a neighborhood could be mitigated by a few token amenities. The villagers of Upper Rime back home in England wouldn't have been so easily silenced. Why should a neighborhood in Queens be any different?

''Naturally, I'd go myself if I were there,'' Carolyn Sue said. ''Nobody ever called me a coward.''

Margaret imagined the reaction of an angry protest group, one of whose members had been murdered, upon seeing Carolyn Sue emerge from her limousine wearing her Maximilian sable with her golden hair piled high and her fingers bedecked with diamonds. The knee-high Ferragamo boots alone would drive them to a frenzy. No, Carolyn Sue Dennis Castrocani Hoopes was not the ideal good fairy come to offer gifts to a sullen crowd of tough blue-collar residents of a neighborhood in the process of being demolished.

''I don't know that I would make a good representative for you,'' Margaret said. Her upper-class British accent would surely be as offensive as Carolyn Sue's down-home drawl, although Margaret knew enough to leave her mink at home.

''Please,'' Carolyn Sue said. ''I feel real bad, and I want to do something nice. I could see that you were taken on by the company as a consultant, so you'd be like an employee. We'd pay you out of our contingency funds—you'd be our public relations representative. I like that!''

Margaret hesitated. She could use the money, and Carolyn Sue had far more than she needed.

"I suppose I could run over tomorrow evening," Margaret said, "if you give me the details."

"That would be jes' grand! I know there's a fax machine somewhere around this hotel. I keep getting this stuff from my offices, and Ben has to keep in touch with all his boys in Texas. . . ." Now that Carolyn Sue had gotten her way, she lapsed into her folksiest down-home accent. "Ah'll send up the information to y'all, and you call me if there's any little ol' thing you don't understand. Ah'll jes' stick by the pool all day tomorrow in case you want to reach me. Why, here's my handsome boy now, lookin' all tan and wonderful. Paul, honey, it's Lady Margaret up in New York. She's goin' to help us out."

Prince Paul Castrocani came on the line. "She started to work on me to do whatever she has convinced you to do," Paul said. "I refused. But politely, as I do not wish to have my holiday terminated. I remember the day you and I visited Queens. I did not find it a pleasant experience. I fear this will be even less pleasant. It sounds dangerous to me."

"It's going to be all right," Margaret said. Then she had an alarming thought. "I say, Paul, do you suppose your mother's people actually did murder this woman?"

"My mother," Paul said seriously, "is not someone I would care to oppose in a matter of business, but I do not believe that murder is one of her options. I may be optimistic in this. I cannot speak for the people of Queens."

"I'll keep a taxi waiting outside while I say my piece, so I can be free of the place immediately if matters don't go well."

Lady Margaret Priam seldom had any doubt that she could handle almost anything, even events in a part of New York City where she rarely had occasion to visit and only passed through on her way to LaGuardia or Kennedy airports. In fact, she was beginning to be rather keen about the adventure.

"It seems quite simple. How bad could it be?" she said

to Paul. Then the line crackled fiercely, and her question echoed back to her: "How . . . bad . . . ?"

She thought she heard Paul say, "Nothing the *principessa* does is simple. *Ciao, cara.*"

Chapter 3

A fax from Carolyn Sue, several pages long, began spilling out of Margaret's fax machine late in the afternoon as she was dressing for a reception for members of the committee to which she had agreed to lend her name. Although she was hazy about the worthy cause that would benefit from the committee's work, her dear friend Dianne Stark was the chair, and Margaret hadn't wanted to refuse her the glamour of an English title on the committee list.

Margaret paused to scan the fax. The first sheet was filled with Carolyn Sue's extravagant, looping handwriting, which only lacked little hearts and circles to dot the letter *i*. Paul often remarked that his mother remained a blond teenage Texas cheerleader at heart, in spite of her millions and millions of dollars.

"My New York people are *really* fine," Carolyn Sue had written, "but they just might lack the common touch. You know."

Margaret blinked. The Priam family, headed by her brother, the Earl of Brayfield, were nice enough people, well schooled in the social graces, good with horses and servants, and certainly remarkably stoic about living during the winter months in the damp and chilly ancestral home, Priam's Priory, but the common touch? Margaret thought they might be just a bit deficient in that department.

"Sandy Krofft is my vice president in charge of the New York office. Absolutely trustworthy and just plain brilliant businesswise, lots of background in development, but rubs some folks the wrong way. You give Sandy a call and plan your strategy. I don't want this building to become a public relations disaster. I've got to rent that space, and every minute's delay costs me a *fortune* in interest on our development money."

Carolyn Sue had provided the numbers for Sandy Krofft's direct phone line, cellular phone, beeper, an answering service, and the main switchboard number of Castrocani Development. Margaret wondered if Prince Aldo Castrocani, off in a decaying villa in the hills outside of Rome, was aware that his former wife had appropriated his ancient family name for her own purposes. No doubt Carolyn Sue's advisers had outlined the advantages of an ethnic corporate name in a highly ethnic city.

"The meeting is at seven-thirty at the parish hall of Saint Lucy's Church. Sandy will tell you who's in charge now that this Frances Rassell is dead."

Margaret fastened a hefty strand of faux black pearls around her neck and stood back at the mirror to see how she looked. Not bad, even if the necklace was only a Chanel knockoff. She was certainly not as emaciated as her fellow committee members would be. She had decided to wear a bold black- and red-checked jacket over a red dress, so she would stand out smartly among the inevitable little black dresses everyone else would be wearing.

So Sandy Krofft was difficult. Well, any number of corporate vice presidents had succumbed to Margaret's charming ways. No real problem there.

Margaret looked at the rest of the faxed pages. Several were bleary, almost illegible, copies of news stories that gave the first hint of development plans in a quiet Queens neighborhood, about the first small voices of protest, then somewhat louder as dissatisfied residents found supporters, and a couple of inflammatory columns written by a popular muckraker who claimed a special affinity with "the little people." Finally, there was an item from yesterday's paper about the murder at the site of Carolyn Sue's building-to-be. Evidently the efficient Sandy Krofft had seen to it that every scrap of the lastest news was sent to Carolyn Sue under her palm tree.

There was a lengthy press release announcing the beginning of construction of an architecturally innovative project from Castrocani Development—apartments, office space, an arcade of boutiques, everything (apparently) the good citizens of Arcadia didn't want.

Margaret decided she must ask Carolyn Sue how she'd gotten into high-rise construction. It was one thing to own a piece of a Manhattan hotel (the exclusive Villa d'Este), a few apartment buildings (including Paul's rent-free Chelsea place), and the odd bit of land for investment purposes. Major development from the ground up was something else.

The next to last sheet was one of Poppy Dill's "Social Scene" columns: the fabulously rich and social Texan Carolyn Sue Hoopes, whom everyone in New York adored, was building a grand new building right here in their city— and Poppy was already looking forward to reporting on a glamorous opening-day party. Of course, Poppy was always eager to stay abreast of the social side of Carolyn Sue's ventures.

Margaret picked up the final slippery fax sheet, an afterthought from Carolyn Sue in which she named a figure for Margaret's services that made her gasp. Then she read the numbers again slowly. What kind of trouble did Carolyn Sue think her project was in to offer to support Margaret in comfort for a year or two? There was more to be learned.

A fast telephone call was in order before she departed for the reception. "Hello, Poppy? Margaret Priam here."

"Margaret, it's been too, *too* long since you've called or

visited. Lonely old ladies like me begin to think they've been forgotten by all their friends.''

Margaret laughed as she glanced again at Carolyn Sue's fax. Poppy Dill might never leave her comfortable East Side apartment to gather the hot social news she wrote up for her newspaper column, but friends and informers, press agents and social and fashion queens of every sort beat a path to her rosy boudoir to spill everything worth reporting, as well as much that could never be told.

''Poppy, I'm going to a reception for the committee Dianne Stark is chairing. I suppose you know all about it? Good. I forgot to ask what the charity was, and I don't want to look the complete fool.''

Poppy sniffed. ''Not as déclassé as poor Helene Harpennis's Adjuvant Youth, but not top drawer. I believe it's going to be difficult to arouse enthusiasm for the Florida manatees here in New York, but conservation is very trendy. Since simply everyone is doing the Brazilian rain forests, I suppose it has to be the poor manatees. Dianne will be hard-pressed to make it sound terribly worthy.''

Margaret had passed through Palm Beach often enough to have been made aware of the plight of the manatees, but she concurred that they were a doubtful inspiration for an outpouring of tightly held charity dollars.

''I was surprised that Dianne took it on,'' Poppy said. ''She's never struck me as the bossy chairlady type. But one assumes she's seeking solace, keeping busy, now that the bloom seems to be off her marriage.''

''No!'' Margaret said involuntarily. ''Not Dianne and Charlie!''

''There have been rumors,'' Poppy said. ''*Not* that I would repeat them. It happens all the time in our set: wealthy older man, younger wife, but then there's an even younger dolly up and coming. I have *no* idea who it could be.'' Poppy paused expectantly, and Margaret understood that she was waiting for Margaret, as one of Dianne's good friends, to enlighten her.

"I had lunch with her only last week," Margaret said, "and she never said a word."

"I feel simply terrible," Poppy said, "but you *will* tell me when you know anything." Poppy's need to know far outweighed her sympathy for the marital woes of the rich and social. "Charlie is *so* rich and *such* a nice man. And Dianne is . . . quite a lovely person." Poppy never forgot that Dianne had been a flight attendant before marrying Charles Stark.

Margaret decided it was time to get to the real point of her call. "I suppose you know all about Carolyn Sue's construction project in Queens."

"What there is to know," Poppy said, then added with considerable delight, "That murder! Of course! One of the lads at the newspaper tipped me off about it, or I wouldn't have noticed. I should have realized that Carolyn Sue would turn to you. You'll have it cleared up in a minute. What a story!"

"No, no. It's not like that. I shall not have anything to do with the murder, so please don't print anything. Carolyn Sue merely asked me to speak to the neighborhood group that's opposed to the building. I'm supposed to be in touch with someone named Sandy Krofft at the New York office, but I thought you might know something useful. Carolyn Sue has offered me an astonishing sum to soothe the injured feelings of the neighborhood. She thinks I have the common touch."

"Now, I know absolutely *nothing* about Carolyn Sue's business," Poppy said, "but I do think you're going to find Sandy Krofft most interesting. A challenge." She laughed a merry little laugh. "I do happen to know something of that neighborhood. Arcadia has become quite the gentrified little community. I've actually met a couple of people who live there. Professional people, even a little snip of a girl who feeds me column items. And those struggling artists and actors who are always looking for places they can afford. Still, it's *quite* another country, not at all like us."

Poppy made "us" sound as though the gossip and rumors seeping along Park Avenue and Fifth were terribly significant in comparison to the upheaval Carolyn Sue was causing across the East River.

Chapter 4

"*Peter! I'm* home!" Rebecca Wellington dumped her briefcase in the entry of their duplex on one of the halfway decent streets in Arcadia, Queens, and called down the hall to the study, where she presumed her husband, home early, was reading his interminable legal briefs. "Peter?" she called up the short flight of stairs to the living room on the second floor.

"I'm on the phone," Peter called down from above. "About the meeting tomorrow."

"The phone, the phone," Rebecca muttered under her breath. She wished she could rip it out. It always brought her trouble.

Rebecca slipped out of her heavy-duty city woman's Reeboks and went into the ground-floor bedroom. She'd been jumpy and irritable all day, and now Peter was going to start about this neighborhood nonsense. It was one thing to be a high-powered female public relations executive, not yet thirty, attractive—and moderately successful. It was something else to be tired and frazzled at day's end and get no sympathy from her husband. Now she had to change clothes and head back to Manhattan. At least when she got to the reception, she'd be surrounded by all those rich social types, and she could relax. Some of them were really lovely people,

18

and the life they led was something to dream about—travel all over the world, beautiful designer clothes, fantastic houses and apartments. She and Peter never seemed to have enough money. He said not to worry, but she knew that if he had more ambition, he would have a good chance of being made a partner in his law firm. Instead he wasted his time being a do-gooder, telling their neighbors how to beat the system. She was the one who was working herself to death.

An incipient headache stirred behind her forehead. She wished she could lie down for a while. She really needed something to bolster her spirits.

"Hi, sweetheart," Peter said. "Hot news. Rumor has it the corporation is sending a big guy to speak to us at the meeting tomorrow. Frances's death shook 'em up, which reminds me: we've got to find out about her visiting hours."

Rebecca felt herself becoming incensed. "I didn't like her; she didn't like me. She spied on people and spread gossip. I thought that once she was dead, that would be the end of her."

"Calm down," Peter said. "I know Frances was difficult, but she meant well. Why are you so jumpy tonight?"

"I'm all right. Don't nag." She turned to him, and their eyes met. He was gazing at her with that mixture of soppy adoration and concern that made her want to scream.

Finally he asked, "Are you okay, hon?"

"I am absolutely dead, Peter. You can't imagine what my day was like, and now I have to call a car and pick up Casey to leave for this reception in an hour." Rebecca looked at herself in the full-length mirror on the closet door. Stripped down to slip and stockings, she thought she might have put on a couple of pounds. "I ought to jog more."

"I don't like you out alone at night," Peter said.

"I can take care of myself." She'd finally gotten used to the neighborhood. Now she scarcely noticed the long blank rows of brick warehouses on the side streets and overgrown vacant lots, where feral dogs watched her from the tangled weeds. "Anyhow, I don't have time tonight."

"Or tomorrow night," Peter said. "The meeting."

"I don't *care* about that meeting."

"Civic responsibility," Peter said predictably.

"Borrrring," Rebecca said. She could see Peter's reflection as he stood in the doorway with his slicked-back blond hair and those round wire glasses he must know were passé. The top button of his shirt was unbuttoned, and the knot of his red tie was loosened. Didn't he realize that red wasn't a power-tie color anymore? She was growing more irritated by the second. "And I'm beginning not to care about this house. Why did we ever move here?" She knew the answer: Peter had good real estate connections, so they'd bought the old row house for a comparative song. He said it was a great investment, the neighborhood had a future. On and on.

"You used to like the idea. A place to fix up, easy commute to the city, the rental apartment on the third floor, room for my workshop in the basement, the garden for you out back."

"Peter, don't start. You've barely set foot in the basement for weeks, and I'll never have the money—or the time—to remodel the way I want to and order all those gorgeous plants and bulbs in the catalogs."

Nothing was going right lately. Things at the firm were too tight to think about the luxury of taking days off, not even weekends. Everybody was competing to get a piece of shrinking publicity budgets. Too many society types were hiding out in their multilevel co-ops until it was safe to don their extravagant plumage freely and openly. If she could land a big commercial account for herself, she'd be set. She'd leave her firm if the deal were good enough.

"Peter, we really must get our own car," she said. "And I'm going to need some money. I hate charging clothes at boutiques. It's so common."

Their eyes met again in the mirror. He nodded. It was so easy. Sometimes she wondered if she still loved him.

Tommy Falco blinked blearily as the elevated subway train screeched to a stop at the Arcadia station a couple of blocks away. He shook the can in a brown paper bag. Empty, but he didn't feel like leaving the shelter of the doorway to get another. The doorway was in one of the old houses, vacant now, with windows covered with metal sheeting. Somebody said the owner sold out because of the new building going up across the street.

Tommy remembered when Gracie Fogel lived in this house. Didn't he have a crush on her when they were in high school? Nearly thirty years ago, right before he dropped out to go to Vietnam. Bad idea, but too late to worry now.

Tommy wasn't doing bad. His cousin Rita let him have a cot in the basement of her house two streets away from where he sat, but he had to keep out of her way and especially out of the way of that guy Ernie she was married to. Sure, Tommy didn't like to work, but name one person who did. Try telling that to Ernie. Tommy liked to buy a few beers at the corner bar and sit on the street watching life happening. And death.

He thought back to two nights ago. Three nights? He'd seen it happen, sitting right here where he was now.

Frances Rassell had come walking down that street and had stopped over by the fence. Somebody came to meet her. Not tall, not really tall, anyhow. He didn't know who it was, but he'd seen what had happened. Frances lying on the ground, the murderer looking through her bag, then sending her down into the hole. He'd watched the murderer walk away as if nothing had happened. Tommy had gotten out of there. He wasn't going to take a look at Frances Rassell's dead body and risk having the cops say he did something to her. She'd made trouble for him a few times, starting back when he was a kid.

Tommy felt in his pocket and found two ones and some change. It was early. Maybe somebody at Larry's Bar would buy him a drink. He could see what people were saying about old Frances.

Out of the corner of his eye, he saw a sudden burst of light, like a camera's flash. But it was only a headlight catching a window down the street. A van raced past. A few seconds later, he heard a crash, as if somebody had thrown bottles at a stone wall. A lot of that stuff was going on lately.

* * *

In the small top floor apartment of Peter and Rebecca Wellington's house, Arthur Cramdell sat at his computer and tried to compose at least one telling line of poetry.

All he could think of was how much he had loathed Frances Rassell and how glad he was that she was dead.

> *Dead, dead, eternally dead.*
> *And I am very glad, he said.*

Arthur looked at what he had typed and deleted it. No point in leaving electronic evidence to indicate his monumental hatred of the woman.

The phone rang. It was a friend from his old Manhattan neighborhood inviting him to dinner tomorrow.

"No, I won't be able to come over to the city," Arthur said. "I must go to a meeting here to celebrate the death of a truly horrendous woman."

A nostalgic longing for his old life in Greenwich Village came and went: the life of the city right outside his door. A nearly anonymous life, where nobody spread spiteful gossip and personal lives were just that. Personal. Secrets stayed hidden. Arthur liked Arcadia all right; it was cheaper than Manhattan. Peter pretended he'd done Arthur a big favor by renting to him, and it had started out okay. Then Frances Rassell had heard something from somebody and couldn't wait to spread her poison, just because he was an outsider. Even though she was dead, the effects lingered. Well, he had one or two things to say about her that he'd kept quiet about. He might just start talking.

Arthur Cramdell liked knowing a lot more about what was happening in Arcadia than his neighbors knew. The real estate management company where he did word processing seven hours a day to support himself and his dreams had no connection with Castrocani Development, but the partners were sharp. They knew everything that was happening in the city, even if nobody was talking openly about it. And both of them had secretaries who didn't know the meaning of "confidential." They liked Arthur—quite nice-looking and polite, always helpful, willing to type up letters and memos on his word processor when the secretaries needed to go shopping for a big date or have their hair done. He paid attention to the documents that crossed his desk. He listened to the office gossip, of which half of one percent turned out to be true.

He looked around his little apartment. It was almost too quiet, even for a fledgling poet. He wondered how Rebecca would feel if he got a cat. She'd probably raise hell, and Peter would go along with her. She had no love for Arthur.

Arthur stood up and went to the windows that overlooked the street in front of the house.

Rebecca was just leaving the building. A private cab was waiting in the street. Arthur saw her speak to the driver and then walk briskly toward the corner. The car waited, and a couple of minutes later she was back. He shook his head and went back to his computer.

Yes, he had plenty of things to talk about if he chose to.

"Those people think we're scum. Think we don't read the newspapers, watch TV. Think we don't know when they're out to make a lot of money off us. Who do they think we are, who do they think they are—are you listening to me, Ernie?"

Rita Powers paused for a breath and slammed her heavy coffee mug down on the table in front of her husband.

Ernie looked up briefly from the sports pages of the *Post*. "You finished? Good. Now put a lock on that lip. What's for supper?"

"They're out there murdering our neighbors." Rita was becoming shriller. "Just before she got killed, Frances was telling me about the crazies moving into the neighborhood. She told me these dangerous radicals are out to ruin decent people's lives, just so's they can have some big fancy building, bring in all these little secretaries with their short skirts, these city people renting apartments, and tear all the old buildings down. They're throwing garbage on our streets to scare us away. Next thing, they'll be beating us up. It's a plot. . . ."

Rita trailed off when Ernie put his newspaper aside and glared at her.

"I don't know who this 'they' is you're talking about, but I did know Frances," he said. "Went to school with her kids. At least with the mean one, Alice. I ain't never had any quarrel with Frances Rassell, but if she was dumb enough to go out and get mugged and killed, it ain't my problem. And she liked sneaking around and spreading rumors to make herself look good. Damn double agent, if you ask me." Ernie had a taste for spy stories. He stood up.

"Where you going now?" Rita demanded.

"Promised to fix a door lock. Put it off as long as I could."

"What door?"

"Just down the block. The lady that takes the photos, the one who moved into Patsy's building. He's off someplace; somebody told her to see if I could do it."

"Is that a fact? The cute little number with the curly hair and the tight jeans? Miss Manhattan over here slumming? Taking pictures of everybody, whether they like it or not. I'd like to know what for."

Ernie didn't bother to answer. He could fix about anything, and this Casey Teale *was* kind of cute. Not that she was likely to come on to him, a guy in his fifties, but at least she wasn't a screaming nag like Rita.

"You coming with me to that meeting tomorrow?" Rita asked as he opened the door.

He shrugged. "Don't mean anything to me one way or another if they build that thing. Guys are telling me this property will be worth something. I can sell out and move out to Bayside." He turned back at the door. "And if I do, that bum Tommy ain't coming with us, you hear? I want my supper when I get back."

Ernie pulled on his jacket and picked up the bag of tools he always left by the front door. He headed down the street toward the three-story house with a wrought-iron gate where

Casey Teale had taken up residence a couple of months ago in the second floor apartment.

Lights were on in the houses all along the street as darkness fell. The neighborhood had sure changed in the past few years. Through one uncurtained window he could see a gigantic painting of a nude woman—a woman with green skin. Had to be that artist fellow with the beard and the three big gray dogs with those weird blue eyes. He could hear a racket coming from the place next door. Rock musicians, they called themselves. He called them punks with earrings and tattoos. People were saying they were to blame for the troubles around here, but nobody could prove it. More likely it was these druggies who had been showing up lately. Somebody was selling stuff on the dark streets where there weren't any houses. He'd talked to guys who'd seen it happening. Then there were the hookers moving in. He'd seen them standing in doorways, having coffee at the all-night diner. He kept clear of them; somebody told him some of them were really men. He wouldn't be sorry to leave the neighborhood.

Ernie stopped and faced his disappointment. Casey Teale, with a big camera bag slung over her shoulder, came down the steep steps of her building and got into a car that was idling in the street. The car passed him, and he saw Casey in the backseat with that pushy dame from the next block, the one with the lawyer husband.

He'd have to fix the lock another time. Back to Rita. He thought about stopping in at Larry's Bar for a beer and then thought better of it. More than likely, Tommy would be there, and he didn't need that. He headed back home and saw that the lights were on at Frances's place. Rita said that her daughter, Alice, was in from the Island for the funeral. Married that Italian guy, Pirelli, years ago. More likely, Alice was looking for anything in the house worth taking away with her.

Ernie smiled to himself. Frances had it coming to her. He hoped Rita had something decent for supper. There was probably a hockey game on TV, so he wouldn't have to listen to her.

* * *

Alice Rassell Pirelli wasn't shedding many tears for her late mother. She sat at the polished oak dining room table and made a neat pile of bank statements and documents that Frances had hidden away in cupboards and dressers around the house.

Ma had done all right for herself, Alice thought. She examined the box of jewelry she'd come across upstairs. Junk mostly, but the bank stuff was something else.

She didn't waste much time on the things her mother had saved from the old days, albums of family photos and the high school yearbooks for herself and her two brothers. Alice looked at an envelope of glossy photos but didn't recognize anyone but Ma. They were recent —some of the start of the new building, some kind of arty nighttime shots. There was a ton of stuff put away in the closets upstairs and down in the basement. It was going to take forever to clear out the place.

Alice tried to calculate how long it would be before she and her two brothers could put the house on the market. How much could they get for it? She knew somebody she could ask privately. Somebody who would be interested in a fast deal, good money.

She'd been nagging her husband about putting in a swimming pool like the neighbors'. Now she could do it herself. Maybe take one of those cruises. Good old Ma.

Chapter 5

*I*t *was* dark when Margaret arrived at the spacious older apartment building on East End Avenue along with a crowd of fellow committee members, many of whom were descending from their limousines. Margaret had taken a bus up First Avenue: Carolyn Sue's promised largess was not yet in hand.

Painfully refined voices floated through the cold evening air: "Margaret, how lovely to see you. . . ." "We must talk. . . ." "Darling, you're looking divine. . . ." "*Love* your hair. . . ."

Women predominated. The male spouses coerced into attending tended to band together. Those men who had actually consented to lend their names to the committee either looked pained that they had said yes to Dianne Stark's pleas (doubtless after calculating the value of good will from a rich and powerful man like Charles Stark) or were pleased as could be that they were there.

Vast elevators thrust them silently upward and spilled them out into a broad, carpeted hallway. A maid took their coats; a small, dark man served them drinks. Margaret spotted Dianne surrounded by admirers and looking far too radiant for one in the alleged throes of wedded woes. Perhaps she was merely pleased that this affair was not taking place at

27

her apartment but at the residence of another very affluent committee member who liked to show off her illegally acquired pre-Columbian gold artifacts and the case of Egyptian scarabs looted in the course of a luxury cruise down the Nile.

Never one to put off until later what could be asked right now, Margaret headed for Dianne to test Poppy's rumor about trouble in her marriage.

"Oops, sorry." A young woman with short, curly, reddish hair, dressed in unadorned black, grinned apologetically as a flash from her camera went off in Margaret's eyes. "I was trying to get a shot of that group over there."

"The chairlady," Margaret said. "No harm done."

Margaret watched the other woman react to the sound of a proper English accent. Like all good society photographers, this one was well aware of New York's Anglophile obsessions. The right accent made all the difference, and even better if it emerged from the mouth of a presentable-looking woman with an upright carriage and an air of aristocratic assurance. Margaret was all of that, so the photographer said, "Let me get a couple of shots of you. . . ." The young woman looked over the crowd. "Know anybody you'd like to be in a photo with?"

"I know them all," Margaret said. "But there's Charles Stark." She waved him over. "Come be preserved for posterity with me, Charlie."

Charles Stark looked not at all like a dissatisfied, wandering husband, but to rise so high in the world of business and finance, one surely had to be something of a dissembler. Here he was with finely barbered silvering hair, smooth, healthy skin, and a very expensively tailored dark suit.

"My pleasure, Margaret," he said, "and then we'll get my wife into a picture."

Flash. Flash again.

"Thanks," the photographer said.

"And you are . . . ?" Another young woman had appeared, notebook in hand. This one was not quite so self-effacing as the photographer, neither in her demeanor nor her dress. Many hours of devoted shopping at Saks and Bloomingdale's and the Madison Avenue designer boutiques had gone into her expensive, if understated, outfit.

"I'm Lady Margaret Priam," Margaret said, "and this is Charles Stark."

"Charlie and I are old chums," the young woman said gaily. She seemed excessively bright-eyed and enthusiastic. The occasion didn't call for quite so much verve. "His wife is *such* a hard worker, *so* gracious. She's spending hours and hours on her committee work. I don't know when she has time for Charlie."

Margaret was suddenly alert. She'd heard that enough times—the wife who neglects her husband in her drive to save the manatees, or help underprivileged children, or preserve grubby but historically significant buildings from destruction. Husband promptly finds solace elsewhere, since he can easily afford it. She hated to think that Poppy's rumors might have some truth to them.

"This is Rebecca Wellington, who's handling the public relations for Dianne's event," Charlie said. "You work hard yourself, Mrs. Wellington."

"It's fun," Rebecca Wellington said, and almost gushed, "when I get to see nice people like you." She turned briefly to Margaret. "I'm sorry. I didn't get your name." She was now beginning to look over the room to locate greener social pastures.

"Lady . . . Margaret . . . Priam," Margaret said distinctly. "I'm on the committee."

"Ah, yes, of course. Excuse us. Quick, Casey. Let's get some pictures of Harry Dowd. *Women's Wear Daily* loves to print him surrounded by his pretty gal pals. See you again *very* soon, Charlie." Rebecca and her photographer went off to line up Harry and a bevy of society belles, chins up, smiles fixed, shoulders back, and feet just *so*.

"What a tiresome woman," Charles Stark said. "I do dislike this first-name basis from someone I scarcely know. She actually invited me to meet her for drinks. Young women certainly have changed. Give me a woman with class like Dianne." Charlie beamed in his wife's direction.

Margaret was relieved that tales of trouble in the Starks' Park Avenue paradise seemed groundless. She was reduced to idle chatter. "I find Harry Dowd quite amazing. I'd love to see his engagement calendar. So many lunches, so little time."

Charlie chuckled. "Can't abide him personally. Thank goodness Dianne is busy enough not to feel she must take him up as a chum."

"About Dianne," Margaret said cautiously. "I've been hearing things."

"Did she tell you?" Charlie sounded surprised.

"No," Margaret said cautiously. "Poppy Dill mentioned . . ."

"Good lord, she doesn't know already, does she?"

"Well . . ." Margaret hesitated, now much more cautious. "She does hear what people are saying."

"It's bound to come out, news like that. Hard to imagine me a new father at my age, isn't it?"

"Ah . . ." Margaret was entirely elated by the announcement. "How lovely. And no, Poppy doesn't know. She thinks she knows something entirely different."

Now Charlie looked somewhat alarmed. "No telling what nonsense that woman will print."

"She won't," Margaret said. "I'll make certain she doesn't. I say, Charlie, do you know someone in the New York corporate world named Sandy Krofft?"

"Mmm. Works for Carolyn Sue Hoopes. Used to work for Zeckendorf or maybe Tishman, or one of those big development fellows. What's your business there?"

"It's about this building Carolyn Sue is erecting somewhere in Queens."

"They were talking about some unpleasantness today at my club."

"A woman was killed at the construction site. Carolyn Sue is troubled by rumors connecting the murder with her company. I gather the neighborhood people are not entirely pleased with Carolyn Sue's attempts to alter their surroundings."

Charles Stark smiled, almost grimly. "Progress will not be halted, and certainly neither Carolyn Sue nor Sandy Krofft is easily turned aside, even by murder. But I don't see Carolyn Sue slaughtering the opposition."

"There's no proof that the death and the building are related."

"But everyone believes it," said someone behind Margaret. The young woman with the camera had spoken, and Charles Stark took the interruption as an opportunity to join his wife. "I live over there," the young woman said. "Look!" She pointed toward the tall windows facing the East River. Roosevelt Island and beyond it Queens twinkled with domestic lights. Except for some apartment buildings on the opposite side of the river, the only significant building was the massive Citicorp tower downriver in Long Island City beyond the Fifty-ninth Street Bridge.

"I moved there recently," the photographer said, "but I've been visiting the neighborhood since before they broke ground."

"I see. I didn't introduce myself. I'm . . ."

"Lady Margaret. I heard. Rebecca and her husband live there, too. That's how I ended up in that neighborhood. I've done a lot of photo work for the public relations firm she works for. I'm Casey Teale." She gestured around the room. "I don't really do this." She grinned. "I'm a serious photographer. Artist with a capital A. Right now, I'm working on a photo essay on the changing scene over there—the old-timers, the newcomers who've been buying up the old houses, and now comes this monstrously inappropriate building. Fascinating. Scary, too, when you realize how remote corporate entities can change the life of a community." She paused. "Change isn't the right word. Kill its soul, smash its body, and sweep away the remains."

"Indeed," Margaret said, taken aback by the bitterness in her voice. "It's difficult to get a feel for it all from this side of the river."

"I do this social stuff to pay the bills," Casey said.

Margaret thought of Carolyn Sue's promised bounty. "How true for many of us," she said.

Casey gave her a long look that clearly said, "Don't kid me, lady. You're born and bred to this kind of life." Margaret was pretty sure Casey Teale did not think that "this kind of life" had much redeeming social value.

"Rebecca calls," Casey said. "Who is that frightful-looking woman she's cornered? How do these women decide what looks good on them and make such terrible mistakes?"

"I believe they rely too much on the kindness of the strangers who run boutiques and hair salons," Margaret said. "She's just another one of us who is deeply concerned about the plight of the Florida manatees."

"Haven't you heard?" Casey said. "Manatees are out, recycling is in. They've changed the thrust of this benefit to Stem the Styrofoam. As if that will feed some sick baby in a tenement."

"I shouldn't imagine anyone in this room has ever actually thought about what happens to the Dom Perignon bottles after the tulip glasses have been filled," Margaret said.

"Or where the caviar jars go when they're empty."

"Or what becomes of *The New York Times* and *The Wall Street Journal* after they've been read. I say, I shouldn't be here. This committee ought to be composed of maids, butlers, doormen, housekeepers, and perhaps Cook and her helpers."

Casey Teale smiled and suddenly seemed less serious. "Absolutely right." She started toward Rebecca, who was arranging to have Charlie and Dianne flank Harry Dowd, much to Charlie's dismay.

"Wait," Margaret said. "I understand there's some sort of meeting tomorrow in Arcadia."

"Yes . . ." Casey was wary. "How would you know that?"

"I'm to speak. On behalf of the . . . um, developer."

"I see." Casey became grim. "We know all about *that* woman."

"She's quite a delight," Margaret said. "Really."

Casey didn't seem convinced. "I may see you then." Rebecca Wellington's signals were becoming impatient.

"Please don't mention my mission to your neighbor."

"To Rebecca? Between you and me, her interest lies strictly in the possibility of her firm handling the public relations for the new building. She couldn't care less who goes to the meeting. She couldn't care less about anything besides herself and instant gratification."

Margaret herself didn't care much at the moment. Queens was a long way from East End Avenue. She managed to catch Dianne alone. "Lunch tomorrow? You have a lot to tell me."

Dianne looked sweetly guilty. "I couldn't tell you until I was certain. I promised Charlie. One o'clock? Think of a nice place."

"Done. Who is this Rebecca Wellington who seems to have a crush on your husband?"

"Her," Dianne said, and shrugged. "The 'I adore older men' school of career advancement with no limit to the services she is willing to provide. Not to worry. She seems quite competent at her job. Charlie finds her tedious."

"I am relieved," Margaret said. "Oh, dear, here comes Harry Dowd. He'll beg me to have lunch in pursuit of an invitation to stay at Priam's Priory."

"Run off and talk to old Madame Rouillion. She'll tell you all the Paris gossip if you're interested."

Margaret was not, but she ran.

The skyline of Queens across the East River continued to twinkle as the masses sat down in front of their television sets and ate their microwaved dinners. Casey Teale shot a few more photos of rail-thin women spearing asparagus and popping shrimp into their mouths, and departed. Rebecca Wellington chatted up social lions and lionesses as though born to be a committee member in her own right. Soon people were looking surreptitiously at their Rolexes and Patek Phillips. Important dinners awaited, an evening at the latest hotter-than-hot musical already sold out for the rest of the century, bags to be packed for a quick trip on the Concorde.

Dianne made a pretty little speech, urging her committee to get out and sell tickets to their all-natural, Styrofoam-free dinner to be followed by a preview performance of the next hotter-than-hot musical to row itself across the Atlantic.

Then the art-filled rooms of the huge apartment emptied quickly. Margaret pledged silently not to speak a word to Sam De Vere about the death of an elderly neighborhood activist in Queens as she taxied downtown to dine with him.

De Vere met her at the door of his Chelsea apartment. Thanks to Carolyn Sue, who owned the building, it was rather grandly furnished, possibly to keep Paul from feeling inferior in a city where his mother was so widely known to be very, very rich.

"Before you say anything," De Vere said, "I had a call from Carolyn Sue today."

"How is she able to track you down when I am never able to get through?" Margaret asked rather crossly.

"She probably knows that police commissioner," De Vere said. "About this business you're involved in . . ."

"I'm not 'involved' in anything," Margaret said defensively.

"She wanted to assure me that you would have no connection with a murder that she claims might be marginally related to her project. And I assured her that you would not."

"That's settled, then," Margaret said. "Where shall we eat? I didn't have a thing at this reception I went to, even though someone seems to have spent a goodly sum on the tidbits they were passing about. The decorative things they are able to do to radishes is quite astounding."

"It's not settled exactly."

"Whatever do you mean?" Margaret thought De Vere looked especially attractive when he was being stern and masterful, and she had an absolutely clear conscience. He did look a bit tired, she thought, and she wondered if he was still mulling over the idea of leaving the police force before he burned out completely.

"I mean that some colleagues in Queens are not convinced it's only marginally related. I made a couple of calls."

"Well, that's too bad for Carolyn Sue, but my function is to be a messenger, a bearer of gifts, as it were, to the aggrieved community."

"Margaret," De Vere said, "I know you. Promise me . . ."

"Anything," she said, "to expedite our departure for dinner."

"I take that as a very serious promise," De Vere said. "And we're not departing. I'm cooking here tonight for us. Since Paul intends to cavort in the Caribbean for an extended period, I'll have plenty of time to do the dishes."

"You amaze me. It never occurred to me that you could cook."

"After my marriage evaporated, I had to learn to fend for myself. I find it more surprising that a blue blood like you knows how to cook."

"Nonsense. I've had to fend for myself, too, as you know perfectly well. I once had a husband who expected a nice joint on Sunday. What's on the cooker?"

"*Arroz con pollo,*" De Vere said. He grinned. "I had a Cuban girlfriend once. About your promise . . ."

"What do your colleagues in Queens think actually happened?"

De Vere hesitated. "They don't think it was a mugger. She had been strangled with a wire, then dumped into the hole at the construction site. Muggers tend not to worry about hiding their victims' bodies. They take the loot and run. In this case, nobody took the loot. She was wearing her rings, a watch; her handbag was with her. They've questioned her neighbors. Some liked her, a lot didn't. She was known as a busybody, into other people's business, and she was especially busy agitating about that building. No suspects, but investigations continue."

"So danger lurks in the depths of Queens. A murderer is on the loose."

"Margaret." There was a note of warning in his voice. "I know you couldn't turn Carolyn Sue down, but I want you in and out of this meeting, and that's the end of it. Nothing more.''

"I assure you, I don't want anything more."

"Good. And just to make certain, I'm coming with you."

Chapter 6

Tommy Falco had an idea.

He didn't often indulge in thinking, largely because the life he led didn't require much thought.

Tommy lay on his stomach under a derelict comforter atop the ratty sheets Rita begrudged him for his cot in the basement and slowly made his way along a cobwebby mental path.

One of the guys at Larry's Bar last night—he forgot who—had said that the cops had been asking around about Frances. Who didn't like her, who could have killed her. They'd started talking to people who hung out around the neighborhood and might know something or have seen something.

"No cops talked to me," Tommy had said as several pairs of eyes turned toward him. Nobody hung out as much as he did. "Maybe they should. They'll be surprised how much I know." Now they were all paying attention, but only for a minute. They knew old Tommy. "If they tried leaning on me, I'd get a lawyer," he added. "I got rights, you know. When I was in Nam . . ." He'd lost their interest. He was starting to feel uneasy that maybe he'd said more than he should. He left Larry's Bar after one more beer, cadged off some guy who wasn't one of the regulars. A big guy, Italian or maybe Hispanic. He hadn't said much, but he put down

37

the money for Tommy's drink and then kind of winked. For a minute Tommy thought he was one of those queer guys, but he never looked at Tommy again.

Now as day was presumably dawning somewhere above the basement of the old row house, Tommy remembered what he'd said and the idea that had emerged from it.

He knew only one lawyer. He didn't like knowing that kind of guy, with the suit and tie and a job in an office. He'd kept out of serious trouble most of his life, so he didn't have to know lawyers. This one seemed okay. Tommy had talked to him on the street, and Casey knew him.

Tommy got dressed quickly and quietly—no point in letting Rita know he was up. She'd start nagging him about the board money he'd promised; and when was he going to get a real job instead of picking up painting jobs here and there? Ernie says this, Ernie says that. He'd get out of the house before she knew it.

The first thing he saw on the street was a cop car parked on the corner near the bodega where the Latino guys hung out all day long, rain or shine.

The car was unmarked, but Tommy knew it for what it was. Nobody was sitting in it, but he didn't take any chances. He walked in the opposite direction.

It was still early, before eight o'clock. People were on their way to work, heading for the subway station. It was a cold and clear day, with traces of snow on the curbs from the snowfall a couple of days before.

"Hey. How ya doin'?" Tommy spotted Casey Teale as she came out of her house wearing jeans and a bright purple parka, with her big camera bag over her shoulder.

Tommy had liked Casey's looks right from the first day he noticed her. She was friendly, even when she was busy photographing the trucks working on the foundation of the building and the people in the neighborhood. She'd even taken a couple of pictures of him. Talked to him about what he was doing with his life, but she was nice, not a know-it-all.

"You're out early, Tommy."

"You, too." He liked her jaunty walk, those greenish eyes,

the no-nonsense way she had. He didn't like the idea that she was pals with that artist with the dogs, or the lawyer's wife who'd like to kill him with a look. What could he do? He couldn't pick her friends for her.

"Going my way?" she asked. "I'm going to try to get some pictures while there's sun."

"Naw. Well, I'm going that way sort of," he said. "I got to see a guy about some business." He rubbed his hand over his chin and realized he hadn't shaved for two, three days.

"Those boarded-up buildings across from the site have some interesting architectural details I didn't notice before. Nineteenth-century moldings with blank, covered-over windows. Another stage in the demise of the old neighborhood. The light should be about right. Nothing like natural light."

"Yeah," Tommy said. He wasn't sure what she was talking about, but he thought she meant Gracie's old house.

She waited until he fell into step with her and said, "So what do you think about Frances Rassell getting killed?"

Tommy looked at her quickly. She was squinting up into the sky, where a faint vapor trail of a jet heading west of LaGuardia was visible.

"It was too bad," he said cautiously. "These drug addicts."

"You think so?" Casey said. "I don't. Somebody didn't like her making trouble. She did that to a lot of people, I hear."

Tommy had a momentary twinge of panic. "What do you mean? The building and that stuff?"

Casey shrugged. "I never figured out whether Frances liked the idea of this building or didn't like it."

"She ran that committee. . . ."

"Mmm. But she was not a nice woman, Tommy."

"Yeah, well. I know what you mean." He didn't know what she meant, except that Frances hadn't been nice to him once in forty years. "I got to see about my business."

Casey seemed to be only half listening. She was taking her camera out of the bag and looking through it at Gracie Fogel's old boarded-up house. A huge, green truck piled with rubble and dirt from the construction site drove past and made the sidewalk tremble. The driver shouted something at Casey, and she waved good-naturedly.

"Same to you, fella," she said softly. Tommy drifted away to act on his idea, which was beginning to seem less good with every step he took.

"Peter, I really *cannot* waste a second this morning. I have to be at the office in half an hour, and I'm not going to make it. I have to see if Poppy Dill wrote up the reception and get last night's photos from Casey."

"Honey, I only asked if you'd be home in time for the meeting tonight. How long can a 'yes' take?"

"It could take a while," Rebecca said, "because I don't know if I will be, and I can't take the time to discuss it. Harry Dowd asked me to drinks to talk about handling some press relations for him. What a coup that would be. I would have told you last night, but you were asleep when I got home."

"It was pretty late. I fell asleep waiting for you," he said.

"I had to go out to dinner with some very important people."

"Who is Harry Dowd?"

"Oh, Peter. You never pay attention to what I do. Everybody knows him; he knows everybody. You must have seen his name in the columns. He's the best friend of every important woman in the city. Does this outfit look all right? We've got to get better light in this room. I can scarcely see myself."

"I still don't know Harry Dowd," Peter said. "What sort of important women?"

Rebecca faced him. She knew that look. The bland, empty look he put on when he was absolutely not interested in what she was saying but was pretending he was.

"Don't sound so jealous," she said. "He happens to be a very good friend of Carolyn Sue Hoopes. You know who she is. Oh, God, who's ringing our doorbell at this hour?"

She drew aside the heavy curtains that covered the iron

grating on the street-level bedroom windows. "I don't believe it."

"Who?"

"That bum. The one who hangs out on the corner. I see
him all the time at the Korean store buying beer."

Peter looked out. "Tommy Falco. I'll take care of him."

"I'll do it," Rebecca said sharply.

She reached the door ahead of Peter.

"Yes?" Rebecca had perfected the minor art of the icy
stare in the presence of the lower orders, having studied the
experts, the ladies who chaired important society commit-
tees and brooked no nonsense.

She succeeded in flustering Tommy to the point of mute-
ness.

Finally he managed to say, "I got to see Mr. Wellington
on business."

"He's left for the day," Rebecca said. "Call him at his
office."

"I have a few minutes, Tommy," Peter said behind her.
"Come on to the study."

"Oh, *really*," Rebecca said under her breath.

She didn't speak again to Peter before she rushed off to
the subway, hateful although convenient, and was only a little
late to her office.

Arthur Cramdell liked to leave early for work. That way he
could usually avoid most of his neighbors. When he had first
moved here, he'd made an effort to be friendly, but once
Frances Rassell had taken a dislike to him, things changed.
Although he didn't know for sure how she had learned about
him, he didn't want to believe that Peter had said something.

Today when he looked through the glass panel of the door
to the steps to the street, he was surprised to see Tommy
Falco coming out of the Wellingtons' street-level front door.
Tommy was one person Arthur did talk to now and then,
mostly because Tommy didn't draw back nervously from
him. This morning, though, Arthur didn't feel like talking to
anybody, and he let Tommy get half a block ahead before he

followed. He couldn't imagine what Tommy had to say to the Wellingtons.

If I thought Rebecca would hate it if I had a cat, Arthur thought, imagine what she had felt about Tommy in her precious house.

Arthur had planned to stop at the diner on the corner to see if the lethal black brew they called coffee would clear his head, but when Tommy went into the diner ahead of him, Arthur changed his mind.

No, thank you, Arthur said to himself. Coffee in a cardboard cup from the wagon next to the office for me.

Rita Powers ran into Frances's daughter, Alice, at the supermarket checkout counter really early, while buying the milk she'd forgotten the day before. Ernie liked milk in his morning coffee.

"I have it on good authority that the developers are planning a memorial to Ma," Alice said importantly. "That shows they were involved up to their necks. They have a guilty conscience. We're thinking of suing. My brothers are all for it, but my husband doesn't want to."

Although she would have been hard-pressed to put it into words, Rita had a suspicion that big corporations didn't come with consciences, but she had no trouble believing Castrocani Development was guilty of something.

"So it was them. I knew it. Wait till I tell Ernie," Rita said. "He keeps saying your mother met up with a mugger."

"The police know who did it, mark my words," Alice said, "but they're scared to accuse the big boys over there." She tossed her head in the direction of Manhattan. "They'd just as soon let me and my poor family suffer without giving us justice."

Rita made a sort of humming sound of agreement.

"And the stuff Ma squirreled away all these years! Why, she's still got some of Pa's clothes and tools, and drawers full of papers and I don't know what. I have got to get it cleared up before the funeral."

"When is it? Ernie and I will try to make it."

"Saturday, ten o'clock."

Rita knew she'd be going alone. Ernie wouldn't waste his Saturday morning on Frances Rassell.

"Visiting hours at Morrissey's tomorrow and Friday. The police business held things up. My husband's coming in from the Island and bringing the kids. I suppose I shouldn't go to that meeting tonight, what with the death in the family and all, but nothing's going to keep me away."

Rita shared Alice's fanciful tale about the memorial to Frances with Ernie while she poured his morning coffee.

"Nobody's goin' to erect a statue for that old witch," Ernie said.

"Alice says the police know who did it."

Ernie looked at her sharply. "Alice always talked too much, and she never knew anything except chasing boys and getting caught smoking in the girls' room. Who'd she say it was?"

"The company," Rita said smugly. "Just what I thought. Alice wants justice."

"Alice wants money," Ernie said. "I'm going over to Flushing, see a guy about business."

"Sure you are," Rita said.

Ernie didn't go to Flushing immediately. He rang Casey Teale's doorbell. Once again, he was disappointed. She didn't answer.

His car was parked down the street, an old car of no interest to a car thief. He was unlocking the door when he was cornered by the artist—or rather by those damned blue-eyed dogs of his. Ernie always tried to give the whole pack, man and beasts, a wide berth. He thought the guy was a loony. He had some kind of foreign accent, besides having that beard and those devilish-looking dogs. Still, he'd seen the guy walking with Casey Teale, so maybe he wasn't totally nuts.

"Mr. Powers," the artist said. "Have you heard the news?"

Ernie shook his head. What was this guy's name? Jan? Only it sounded like "yawn" when he said it.

"The police are going to make an announcement tonight about the murder—*and* about all this nasty harassment that's hit the neighborhood."

"Didn't hear that," Ernie said shortly. "I've heard just about every other dumb thing people are saying." He tried to edge away from one of the dogs, which had started nosing around his pants' cuff.

"I happened to talk with the daughter of Mrs. Rassell."

"Alice, yeah. She's got a story for everybody."

"She said she'd been reliably informed that the case has been solved."

"Is that so?" Ernie said. "Only thing I know is these women always get it all wrong. I got to get moving. See you around."

Ernie got into his car. At least none of the dogs had taken a chunk out of his ankle.

Chapter 7

The offices of Castrocani Development were located in a very high-rise building in a very high-rent district in midtown Manhattan. Trust Carolyn Sue to eschew functional, economical space in a less fashionable part of town.

It had been remarkably easy for Margaret to arrange a meeting with Sandy Krofft. A telephone call at one minute past nine was all it took to schedule a meeting at eleven. The receptionist with whom she spoke seemed to have instructions to accommodate Lady Margaret's every whim. Margaret suspected that it was more a case of satisfying Carolyn Sue.

Margaret had decided on severe charcoal gray with a paler gray silk blouse. She wore her mink, naturally. Her own philosophy vis-à-vis animals stopped short of depriving small, vicious beasts of their birthright, a long posthumous existence as a coat. As a final touch, she had slipped on the faux emerald ring that was an enduring memento of a bizarre interlude in Beverly Hills, the land where faux was fact.

At the appointed hour, Margaret pushed open the heavy door of the offices of Castrocani Development.

If Carolyn Sue had used an interior designer for the space, she had still managed to impose her tastes, which in this case

45

ran to the Italian Renaissance, no doubt a tribute to her former life as Princess Castrocani.

There was quite a bit more marble than Margaret had seen in any building outside of a major cathedral and Trump Tower: on the floors, on the walls, on the ceiling. There was a receptionist's desk that Michelangelo might have tossed off on a slow afternoon, with creamy white marble limbs and other body parts forming a decorative frieze across the front. The stiff-looking sofas for waiting businesspeople were covered in dark green watered silk, with ornate golden armrests to match the equally ornate standing lamps. There was even a chandelier of sorts, but happily unlit. Most of the lighting came from hidden sources behind the plump marble *putti* who smiled down angelically from the molding.

A rather impressive tapestry—faded enough to be the real thing—hung behind the receptionist's desk. Margaret looked twice at the large portrait of a fierce-looking clerical gentleman in red robes. Another case of the real thing, this one a Renaissance prince of the Church, an elderly cardinal whom the ancient Castrocani family could perhaps claim as an ancestor. Carolyn Sue may have thought he lent a touch of moral rectitude to a business that occasionally required cutting a few moral corners.

The receptionist was as lush as the surroundings: a truly stunning, young black woman, lavishly endowed and gotten up in a crimson outfit that picked up the color of the cardinal's robes.

"Please take a seat, Lady Margaret," the young woman said without a word from Margaret. "I've indicated that you have arrived."

"Well, yes. Lovely." Margaret found the sofa to be more comfortable than it looked.

"Shall I have an espresso or cappuccino brought? Or an aperitivo?"

"Nothing, thank you," Margaret said. "I'll just admire . . . things."

"It's something to look at, all right." The receptionist almost chuckled, then busied herself answering the discreetly ringing telephone. "Castrocani, good morning . . ." Her telephone voice was deep and sexy.

If Margaret had hoped to chat up the receptionist to get a hint of what Sandy Krofft was like (and she *had* so hoped), that was not to be. The help seemed disinclined to converse. Margaret resigned herself to leafing through the latest issue of *Fortune*, and the usual wait for Mr. Vice President Krofft.

The wide doors beside the receptionist's desk were flung open. The woman who strode in was another glamour girl, this one very blond and very blue-eyed. She wore a curve-clinging pink cashmere suit, and Margaret noticed that her remarkably long nails were painted to match the color exactly. Castrocani Development's job descriptions obviously included some special requirements.

"Lady Margaret, how good of you to arrange to see me on such short notice."

Margaret took the outstretched hand and hoped that her expression did not reveal her shock in discovering that this was Sandy Krofft and not the decorative administrative assistant she had first taken her to be. How typical of Carolyn Sue not to entrust her important affairs to a mere man, who would likely challenge her decisions by some imagined right. That sort of behavior, Margaret understood, was reserved for Carolyn Sue's beloved Ben Hoopes, over whom she had, according to Paul, absolute but well-concealed control.

"How *interesting* to meet you," Margaret said. Poppy Dill had been right: the experience of meeting Sandy Krofft was remarkably interesting. Now Sandy guided her toward the door into the inner sanctum.

"Hold my calls, Dawn, unless it's that idiot architect. What I have to say to him will take thirty seconds. The construction manager can wait until I'm free. I won't be long."

The receptionist nodded. She had a slight, wry smile.

Sandy Krofft kept talking as she led Margaret along the silent, thickly carpeted hallway. "Carolyn Sue tells me she wants you to help clear up our little public relations mess in Queens. Is that possible? I advised her to ignore the whole matter or else bring on board someone who's really experienced in defusing bad PR, but Carolyn Sue is such a softy."

Margaret didn't think that accurately described Carolyn Sue but did not disagree, especially since it was clear that Sandy Krofft did not hold Margaret in high regard.

"I do think murder is something more than a 'little' public relations problem," Margaret said.

"Oh, that . . ." Sandy dismissed an old woman done in in the dark with a wave of her hand. "Here's my office." She ran her exquisitely manicured fingers through her near-platinum hair. "It's a mess. My secretary's wife just had a baby, and he insisted on taking a few days off."

The "mess" consisted of two pieces of paper on a black marble slab set on spindly steel legs. Margaret took it to be a desk as there was also a silver pen in a holder and a space-age telephone on it.

This room was light years away from the Renaissance. It was hard-edged modern, black, white, and stainless steel, with the only relief the multicolored stripes on a slim Murano glass decanter on a table near a group of black leather chairs.

In spite of Sandy's instructions, the phone rang. "Dawn, I told you . . ." She glanced at Margaret. "Even Sandlot calls. Get a number." She turned to Margaret. "Coffee?" Two attractive young people, male and female, carried in espresso in tiny china cups and departed.

"I had no idea," Margaret said, "that Carolyn Sue had such an elaborate organization in Manhattan."

"It's quite new," Sandy said. "She's had an office in Dallas for several years, but when her people started buying up bits of land around New York, we decided it was time to produce income from all that investment."

We. Margaret caught that. "So to produce income, she decided to spend a lot of money building her building."

"It's not quite that simple," Sandy said in a tone that implied she certainly didn't have time to explain the basics of real estate development to a simple soul like Margaret.

"You've worked with Carolyn Sue for some time, then?"

"A while," Sandy said, and turned brisk, setting down

her espresso cup and picking up a thin black leather portfolio from the floor beside her chair. The stage had been carefully prepared in advance of Margaret's visit. "Now, I don't want to take up too much of your valuable time. . . ."

Meaning, Margaret presumed, that Sandy didn't want to waste any time at all on Lady Margaret.

"I assume you feel you ought to know about Frances Rassell," Sandy said. "I told the police that I have no idea what she was doing at the site, but I can't stop people from walking the streets. The security guard who was on duty saw nothing."

"But you did know her. Personally, I mean."

"I had very little direct contact with her. Some letters obviously written by someone else for her signature, one face-to-face meeting with her and a few others from the neighborhood. Grievances, empty threats, the usual business."

"She was definitely opposed to the building, then?"

Sandy smiled faintly. "I had the impression she had a secret longing to share in the glamour our building will bring to the neighborhood. There are others who can see the advantages clearly, but they hesitate to speak out publicly. It's a fairly gritty place. Well, you'll see for yourself if you insist on going to this meeting tonight."

"It isn't really a matter of me insisting," Margaret began.

Sandy looked at her coolly. Margaret read contempt for the interfering ways of Carolyn Sue and her dithery British chum.

"I could handle it perfectly," Sandy said. "I know far more about what's going on over there than I could possibly explain to you."

"Indeed," Margaret said. "And how is that the case?"

"I have people in the neighborhood," Sandy said shortly, and changed the subject. "Carolyn Sue says she has faxed you the background. Now you must understand that the woman's death is totally unrelated to our business. It's the kind of neighborhood that attracts undesirables, and then you never know what these teenage hoodlums will do when they get bored. Off an old lady just for the thrill of it.''

"I understood that it was quite a deliberate murder," Margaret said. "Strangled, no robbery."

"A personal grudge, then. But definitely nothing to do with our building. Nothing. Make that perfectly clear."

That was the party line, then, much as Margaret had expected.

"Carolyn Sue insists that we offer them amenities beyond what we were required to provide by the powers that be. I have a list of what we feel we can offer them to shut them up. We'll build the building no matter how noisy they get, but I want to put a stop to these attempts to make it a media circus."

"Has there been much in the press?" Margaret asked. "I haven't noticed."

"There will be if certain people have their way. All we'd need is a couple of lawsuits or some serious trouble over there." A murder was apparently not serious. Sandy leafed through her papers. "I hate to give up this parcel of land for a park, but I can't talk Carolyn Sue out of it. No problem in setting aside a room in the building for senior citizens. Every building has unrentable space. No furnishings, though. That's their problem."

"The park," Margaret said. "Who will create it, pay for it?"

Sandy Krofft wrinkled her straight little nose in disgust. She was really quite a beautiful woman, about thirty, taller than Margaret, who was not short. But was she the brains or only a front woman? She certainly talked as though she were completely in charge.

"The city is in such lousy financial shape, it will probably only want to contribute some trees, but I'll fight paying for it. The city will be involved somehow. You can't get anything done without somebody from some agency looking over your shoulder." She handed a sheaf of papers to Margaret. "I've written out a statement for you. You don't have to say anything beyond what's down on paper. Carolyn Sue says you'll probably do it nicely enough.''

Thank you, Carolyn Sue, for your vote of confidence, Margaret thought, even as she felt a strong surge of resentment at being condescended to by this tough young woman.

Margaret decided it was time for her to be condescending. ''Miss Krofft, I *do* appreciate your guidance. But please understand that I have *years* of experience dealing with the lower orders. As my father, the late Earl of Brayfield, often said, 'Stand up, say your piece, say it honestly. The people are grateful for guidance in their thinking.' But matters are handled somewhat differently over here, are they not? I hear so much talk of letting people decide for themselves. Such a bore, but we'll see about that, won't we?''

Margaret was quite enjoying her little scene as the arrogant aristocrat telling an offensive young woman a fanciful tale of the way things are done in the feudal lands across the sea.

Reality was quite different; the people in the village of Upper Rime near the Priam estate were reasonably polite to Lady Margaret and on formal occasions were respectful to her brother, the present earl. Otherwise they proceeded to think and do whatever suited them. She imagined that the Queens neighborhood she was about to venture into would behave in the same way, perhaps without the politeness and respect.

Sandy drew back a bit in the face of the preposterous nonsense Margaret had uttered.

''Now,'' Margaret said brightly, ''who is it I should see about arranging to speak?''

''Frances ran the meetings, but you're to look for a man named Peter Wellington. He's an interested newcomer to the neighborhood, basically in the opposing camp but not one of the hotheads. He's actually been quite helpful in smoothing out difficulties. A bright young lawyer. I've told him you'll be there. He'll be waiting for you at Saint Lucy's parish hall.''

Sandy stood up, impatient for her to be gone.

''That's all?'' Margaret said.

"This is a futile exercise in diplomacy, and I've told Carolyn Sue that over and over again," Sandy said. "I'm sure if you're nice to them, tell them what they're going to get, they'll eat it up." She looked at Margaret without hope that she could carry it off, in spite of sounding like the lady of the manor. "I'd just like to keep anything bad out of the papers and everything good in the headlines. It's hard enough to rent space these days. One major firm that was planning to sign a long-term lease for several floors is wobbling. Trouble could ruin the deal, even if we won't open for two years. When will those little people over there learn?"

Margaret took that to be rhetorical. A pretty little park and a gathering place for senior citizens were all very nice, but even "little people" might feel uneasy under the circumstances, especially with an unsolved murder hanging over them.

Eventually someone would solve the murder, and the neighborhood would make the necessary adjustments, with nothing to the detriment of Carolyn Sue, who was basically all right, although rich.

"More espresso?" Sandy did not sound encouraging.

"No, thanks awfully. Saint Lucy's parish hall, is it? Seven-thirty. Peter Wellington."

"Yes. I have the address here and the directions written out for the cab driver. Or do you have a car?"

"I have a driver," Margaret said. "He's a policeman." Then she said, perhaps unwisely, "I suppose you'd prefer having someone other than me handling your public relations. Someone like Peter Wellington's wife, Rebecca. She's a professional and quite . . . strong. On the other hand, that could be something of a problem. Husband opposed, wife eager to work for the other side."

"I don't know what you mean." For the first time, she had Sandy Krofft's undivided attention. "Where did you hear this? Do you know her well?"

"I see her about at these parties I go to, smoothing the way for this charity and that. I thought you were considering her."

"You are mistaken," Sandy said, and Margaret knew she was not. Sandy started to maneuver her out of the office.

The hallways of Castrocani Development remained remarkably silent. Indeed, except for the receptionist and the two servers of coffee, Margaret had had only a fleeting glimpse of a young woman at the end of the hall with a handful of papers.

"Are there other projects besides the building in Queens?" Margaret asked.

"We have various interests," Sandy said. She had stopped being civil, let alone friendly, to Margaret.

"Ah! Is that the building?" They passed an open door, revealing a more lived-in and conventional office with a wooden desk piled high with papers, a long, black sofa, a bank of bookcases, some functional filing cabinets. On a low, square table, looking like a small shrine, stood a model of a building a few dozen stories high, all blue-green glass and reddish beige stone. Patches of green were meant to represent tiny plazas at the foot of the tower, complete with tiny trees and tiny benches for weary workers and apartment dwellers. Margaret did not think the existing residents of Arcadia would be encouraged to enjoy the decorative plazas. The natives would have their own park elsewhere. There was, of course, no indication of the existing surrounding structures. Perhaps in the corporate mind of Castrocani Development, everything had already been swept away in a frenzy of demolition.

It did not appear especially distinguished to Margaret's eyes, but her idea of distinguished architecture leaned toward the clusters of Elizabethan chimneys and gables of Priam's Priory, the Riccardi palazzo in Florence, and the I.M. Pei Pyramide at the Louvre.

"What the hell are you doing here?" Sandy said sharply.

Margaret looked around quickly. A heavy-set, well-dressed man stood in the doorway. He was fortyish, dark-haired, and swarthy, and Margaret noted an ostentatious diamond pinkie ring on his left hand and a scowl on his face.

"I work here, babe," the man said. "What are you doing in my office?"

"Sorry, Johnny." Sandy was immediately conciliatory, perhaps for Margaret's benefit. "You startled me. We were looking at the model. I thought you weren't coming in today."

"I had a change of plans. The Sandlot thing I was working on didn't come off, and . . ."

"Johnny," Sandy interrupted firmly, "this is Lady Margaret Priam, Carolyn Sue's friend. The one who's going to Queens for us."

"Ah. Right." He looked Margaret over. "John Mascarpone. I'm a distant cousin of Carolyn Sue's by way of her old marriage to Prince Aldo. Aldo's father, the old *Principe*, was a relative of my father's. I don't trade on the relationship."

"No, of course not," Margaret said. "How delightful to meet you. Carolyn Sue never mentioned . . . Well, I must be off. Lunch, you know. Such a *busy* day."

Sandy's opinion of Margaret continued to be significantly low, if her expression was any indication: a flighty, upperclass Brit doing the business of a flighty, rich, Texas lady.

"By the way," Sandy said, "Carolyn Sue is having your fee sent from the Dallas office."

"Fee?" Margaret decided to play dumb.

"Didn't Carolyn Sue tell you?"

"Something for my trouble was what she said."

"It's rather more substantial than that," Sandy said.

"Lovely," Margaret said. "I'll buy some new frocks."

Let her continue to think I'm as dim as a doorpost, Margaret decided.

Margaret nodded to Dawn, the receptionist. "It must be interesting to work here," she said. "Such a busy office."

"Not always," Dawn said. "You have a nice day."

Margaret didn't like much of what she'd seen of Castrocani Development, but she would do her duty, with De Vere at her side in the event things turned nasty.

She remembered what Casey Teale had said: "We know

all about that woman." Margaret had taken it as a reference to Carolyn Sue, but of course she had meant Sandy Krofft.

Then like Tommy Falco, Margaret had an idea. Happily, she was more accustomed both to having ideas and to acting on them.

Chapter 8

*M*argaret *did* not go to lunch with Dianne Stark.

She found a telephone booth on a Manhattan street corner with a phone that was still intact and functioning, and she cancelled. She was back in her apartment by noon.

Steel drums were serenading Carolyn Sue on her palm-shaded patio when Margaret telephoned her.

"Sandy Krofft is terrifying," Margaret said. "Wherever did you find her?"

"Why, she has the very best credentials and recommendations," Carolyn Sue said. And then, away from the phone Margaret heard, "Ben, honey, would you ask those boys to hold off on 'Amazing Grace' for just a bitty second while I talk to Margaret?" The music ceased. "She's been handlin' everything very well."

"Do you like her? Do you trust her? Tell the truth."

"Don't have a reason not to trust her. She's not really a *likable* person. What are you sayin'?"

"I was not entirely in agreement with her attitude about the neighborhood, nor am I yet clear about her agenda. She's tough. I can't imagine the lengths she'd go to to protect her interests," Margaret said.

"*My* interests."

"And exactly who is John Mascarpone?"

56

"So you met Johnny. I hired him on kinda as a favor to Aldo." Carolyn Sue continued to have a soft spot for her former husband. "In exchange for the use of the family name." Carolyn Sue was silent for a time, and Margaret thought she heard the sound of Caribbean waves on the beach in the distance.

"Well, I certainly *do* trust *you*," Carolyn Sue said. "You call and tell me everything that goes on tonight first thing."

"I think you're going to have to finance the park as well as give them the land," Margaret said.

"Oh, hell, why not? I got plenty of money."

"Then let's spend it," Margaret said.

"I said I trusted you to do what's right," Carolyn Sue said. "Paul sends his love. He's got a nice gal whose daddy owns most of Montana."

"Ask him to get a figure in square miles," Margaret said. "By the way, what's Sandlot?"

"Well, it's this kind of empty field where little boys play baseball. I'll be looking to hear from you." The steel band started in again, and Carolyn Sue was already easing back in the pleasures of her far-off, sun-drenched world.

The Manhattan telephone directory did not list anything called Sandlot, but the information operator plugged her into an automated voice that gave her a number. As soon as she heard the deep, throaty voice answer, she hung up.

Another automated voice gave her Casey Teale's telephone number in Queens. It was a rash hope that Casey would answer in the middle of a weekday when almost everyone was at work, but since she had indicated that she was employed here and there as a photographer, there was just a chance.

She wasn't at home. Margaret left a message on her answering machine. "Margaret Priam. I met you at the committee do last evening. I plan to visit the construction site today about two. Please meet me if you're free. In any case, I'd rather you didn't mention my plan to visit the neighborhood."

She sighed. Was it a mistake to go over there? She did

have an excuse. The model of the building didn't give her a true picture; it would be dark by the time she reached the meeting. She wanted to know what she was talking about, even if she was expected to follow a script.

Margaret cast aside her elegant suit and silk blouse. She put away the faux emerald ring next to the real one she'd inherited from her mother, the Countess of Brayfield. She put on the jeans she wore to tramp the New Jersey countryside when she and De Vere visited his parents and pulled on high, well-worn leather boots. A heavy black cable stitch sweater and a lightweight anorak would do. She removed her makeup and found a black fisherman's cap. Just the jaunty touch she wanted. She zipped keys, money, and the directions to the neighborhood into a pocket of the anorak.

At the door, she turned back and hunted up the pair of reflecting aviator sunglasses she never wore because she didn't like the way they looked on her. They were, she decided, the perfect finishing touch for her disguise. If Sandy Krofft had "people in the neighborhood," she'd prefer not to have them recognize her after the fact at the meeting tonight.

The taxi driver careened over the Fifty-ninth Street Bridge from Manhattan to Queens with a gleeful disregard for slower-moving traffic. Margaret endured white knuckles in the claustrophobic backseat.

"Look at that. Good, huh?" was his over-the-shoulder comment as they reached the midpoint of the bridge high above the East River. The view downriver toward New York Harbor was quite grand: Manhattan's posh apartment buildings edging one side of the river, with the monolithic rectangle of the United Nations beyond, and further, a glimpse of the Williamsburg, Manhattan, and Brooklyn Bridges tying Manhattan and Brooklyn together with strands of decaying steel. On the other side were jumbles of low buildings, the immense Citicorp tower, the smokestacks of the Con Edison plant, and the puffy white domes of indoor tennis courts on the river's edge.

She'd heard that more slushy snow was on the way, but the sky remained clear and pale, icy blue.

The taxi flew down the ramp at Queens Plaza into a mass of vehicles that didn't seem to be moving at all. Margaret peered cautiously over the backseat to locate the driver's name in case the worst happened, as seemed likely. Abdul something. No doubt he'd learned his driving skills in the action-packed streets of some dusty Middle Eastern city and had transferred them unaltered to New York.

As she resigned herself to a wretched fate—with no identification, she remembered, to put a name to her remains—the traffic moved at the change of a light. Miraculously they glided easily through the tangle of the plaza onto side streets, and quite soon, they lurched to a stop beside a chaotic jumble of wooden fences and heavy orange plastic netting. A truck climbed the steep incline from the hole in the ground to the street.

"This is it," Margaret said, and wondered if she'd ever see home again. If worst came to worst, she'd take the subway back to Manhattan; the elevated tracks were visible in the distance over the roofs of the three-story houses.

The site was bigger than she had imagined, although only a few construction workers in work clothes were gathered near the open gate to the pit. Long steel rods were being unloaded from a flatbed truck and piled up at the edge of the site. A muscular young man in a sleeveless padded vest and hard hat was waving an orange flag to direct nonexistent traffic. There was no sign of Casey Teale, but it was still a while before two.

The old-fashioned stainless-steel diner on the corner looked like a warm place to wait. She put on her aviator glasses and headed for a choice of oily coffeelike liquid or hot water with a flimsy tea bag in it.

It was not long past the lunch hour, but only one person sat at the counter. Two booths were occupied, one by a dejected, seedy-looking man nodding over a coffee cup and the other by two middle-aged men in animated conversation. Margaret took a booth far away from both.

"You need a menu?" The bored waitress in sensible shoes and black uniform with a white apron shuffled over, clutching a menu she seemed unwilling to share with Margaret.

Since Margaret had managed only a few mouthfuls of salad while getting ready for her foray into the outer boroughs, she was hungry.

"What is good?" she asked without much hope of a valid answer. She felt as though she were in another country, so she thought it wise to inquire about the local specialties.

"Here? People seem to like Nicky's omelets. Feta cheese, that's like Greek cheese. These guys are all Greeks, you know. I wouldn't touch the fries myself. Try a couple slices of tomato."

"And tea," Margaret said.

"You got it. You English?"

"Australian," Margaret said quickly. She'd forgotten to camouflage her accent. "Do you live around here?" She tried to alter her vowels to match her fiction, then realized it didn't matter.

"Hey, Nick! Feta omelet, hold the fries," the waitress yelled over her shoulder to an idle short-order cook. "Me? Naw. I come from Sunnyside."

"So I suppose you don't care one way or the other about this building I see going up."

"I sure do care," the waitress said. "Plenty of business from the construction guys, first of all. Lots of them tip real good. Then there's all the people going to be working and living in the place. Everybody likes a neighborhood diner, right? So I'm set, unless the boss sells out so they can open one of the fancy 'cafés' or 'boutiques.' Know what I mean?" She jerked her head toward the booth where the two men were still in animated discussion. "That's him, the boss. The light in here bothering you?"

"No. Oh, my sunglasses. I'm in disguise."

"Right." The waitress shrugged. "I'll get your tea."

The tea was bearable, the omelet was delicious, but the tomatoes were pale and markedly untomatolike. One and a half out of three wasn't bad.

"Spiros."

He cast a shadow on the table, a man much bulkier than he had appeared sitting down in the booth.

"You a reporter or something?" He had a lot of very black hair and a bold and bristling mustache. His tie was eye-catching, to say the least.

"Nothing of the sort."

"You were asking Anita questions."

"One or two, out of curiosity. I'm meeting a friend who lives in the neighborhood, and I noticed the construction. May I ask why you're asking?"

Spiros contemplated her, neither friendly nor hostile. "Curiosity, just like you. I get a lot of people coming around with the idea of moving in to make some bucks when the building's up. They look at this place, think they might buy me out. They find out I got businesses in the neighborhood, they ask questions, pretend they're just curious." He squeezed himself into the seat across from her. "Not that you look like one of them. But I get reporters, too, smelling out a story."

"I believe I did read something about a woman being killed." Margaret looked at her watch surreptitiously. She didn't want to miss Casey, but she wanted to hear what Spiros had to say.

"Her. She was just an old dame who lived in the neighborhood. Used to come in here at lunchtime, take up a whole booth by herself, and only order a toasted English muffin and coffee. It's our busy time. We had words once or twice."

"Who killed her?"

Instead of offering an opinion, Spiros shrugged and said, "You like the neighborhood? I got a couple of buildings with apartments to rent. The place could use another good-looking woman." He was almost leering.

"It sounds dangerous," Margaret said.

"It's safe. Old Frances got in the way of somebody who didn't like what she was up to. I was talking to her daughter today; she thinks the developers wanted to shut her up."

"Surely a big corporation doesn't resort to murder."

"What do they care? It's their ball game. I adjust to what's happening. I got a big investment in this neighborhood, like to keep an eye on what's going on. But quietlike. Frances wasn't quiet. Some people around here, they can't face changes. My ancestors back in the old country had this philosophy: 'Everything changes,' he said." Spiros repeated the words in what Margaret recognized as Greek.

"Heraclitus," she said.

Spiros liked that. "Yeah. He was looking at a river going by when he thought of it. He was right. You come around sometime and try Nicky's moussaka. And some days he's got avgolemono for special customers." He winked.

"Egg-lemon soup. Lovely. I shall certainly try to come round again. I really must be going."

If Casey Teale wasn't at the construction site, Margaret would take a stroll around the neighborhood on her own.

The dejected man was still staring down at his coffee cup as Spiros walked with her to the cash register. Spiros made her faintly uncomfortable: too attentive to a stranger, and even though apparently at ease in his own domain, his eyes were everywhere.

Spiros paused to toss a command in the direction of the lone man in the booth. "Tommy. No more refills. Got that?"

Tommy looked up, startled. He was a small man, unshaven and seedy, with a wary, almost frightened look in his eyes.

Spiros held the door for her after she had paid the modest check. "He's one of the neighborhood characters. Vietnam vet. I try to be nice, but you can't let them take advantage. He's been sitting there half the day."

Alone on the street, she saw that the clouds were beginning to move in. The sky was grayish now, and she felt a hint of the coming precipitation. She saw Casey Teale in the distance, huddled up in a purple parka with her back to the orange net fencing.

"I don't understand the secrecy," Casey said. "And those shades make you look like something from outer space."

"I didn't want anyone to recognize me."

Casey was briefly amused. "Are you pretending to be CIA or something?"

Margaret laughed. "Not at all." She took off the glasses and zipped them into a pocket. "I wanted to have a look at the neighborhood, but I didn't want anyone to notice me so they could accuse me tonight of spying. Do you think I'm wrong?"

"Maybe too careful," Casey said. "I won't say a word, and there aren't many people around during the day. Some nosy old ladies and people who don't work in the conventional sense—artists, actors, writers, musicians. The kind of people who are free to go to the noon show of the opening day of a movie and then come back to finish up their freelance assignments."

Casey had a small camera on a strap around her neck. As she spoke to Margaret, she raised it and rapidly shot three pictures of a woman in a shaggy fur coat walking toward the newspaper store on the corner.

"That's Frances Rassell's daughter. She lives out on Long Island, but she's taken up residence in her mother's house a couple of blocks away, probably to plunder the contents."

"Why did you take her photo?"

"Habit. I shoot anything that moves. Whatever looks interesting, tells a story. That reminds me. I loaned Frances some photos I'd like to get back. Shots of one of their protests and " She grinned. "A couple of other pictures she 'borrowed' from me. She called my stuff 'the ugly truth,' but she thought the ones I took of her were pretty good. So—" She gestured widely. "Here's our corner of Queens. It all started out as farmland, with villages at the crossroads. Arcadia turned middle-class a hundred years ago when they built the row houses you still find on some of the streets. Then came factories and warehouses and lots of immigrants—Italians, Germans, Irish, Eastern Europeans. Then Latinos, Filipinos, Indians, Koreans. A few blacks, and now the dreaded yuppies with the money to buy up the old houses and remodel. Back to middle-class."

"Is this building going to be such a disaster, if changes have been going on since the beginning?"

"I don't like what it represents," Casey said. "Look, that row of houses over there had people living, dying, getting married, having children. . . ." She pointed to a row of three-story brick buildings with boarded-up windows. "They'll be gone soon. The new building will alter the way we live here: more people, more traffic, more trendy little shops and restaurants. More people will sell their homes for what outrageous price they can get; more big buildings will appear. I've seen it happen. The little town where I grew up was just close enough to a city to become a bedroom community. It killed my father to see the developers turn the woods into tract housing and the streams funneled into concrete culverts. Malls where the old ice-cream shop used to be, a parking lot covering the old sandlot baseball field."

Margaret looked at her quickly. Casey kept talking. "I understand when the folks who've been in a place all their lives don't like changes. Even the ones who came here more recently and liked what they found don't want it changed." Casey shrugged. "Nothing stays the same, but what bothers me is the high-handed way things are done."

"What do these little people know?" Margaret murmured. Casey frowned, and Margaret added hastily, "Not my words. We have developers in England, too, you know. Sometimes the villages succeed in keeping them at bay, sometimes they don't."

Casey said abruptly, "I don't have much time. We can make a circuit of the construction site. I'll show you where Frances was killed."

They turned down a short, lovely block with neat houses fronted by wrought-iron fences with little patches of earth that would be tiny gardens in the spring. The brickwork and stone were newly pointed, the doors were painted bright colors, and the brass doorknobs were polished. Trees were planted in front of each house at the curb, bare now in winter but promising a shady passage in the heat of summer. Margaret looked up. In a year or two, this pleasant street would be backed by a twenty-story wall of glass and stone, enough to dishearten any householder who had polished his door-knobs and painted his door.

They paused to look through a hole in the fence down into the pit. Cement walls were in place with iron rods protruding from the concrete. A truck was loaded up and ready to depart.

"She was killed on the other side," Casey said, "where the trucks exit."

"I wonder why," Margaret said.

Casey hesitated. "She wanted everyone's approval. She played both sides." Casey was walking faster. "You wouldn't understand. You're protected by money and social position. As are the developers."

Margaret didn't want to argue the point, since she wasn't sure she could convince Casey that she was equally vulnerable to the march of progress and other disasters of modern life.

"What was Frances doing here, do you think?"

Casey shrugged. "It was her neighborhood. I used to see her taking walks at night. It's not as safe as it used to be, but I haven't had any problems."

"Definitely not a mugger?"

"I think she was meeting someone." She hesitated. "Maybe someone from the outside."

Casey eyed a middle-aged woman bundled up in a plain coat, carrying two loaded plastic shopping bags. She chose not to photograph her or a passing pack of teenagers.

"I met Sandy Krofft today," Margaret said. "I suspect from something you said that you must know her."

"She never impressed me," Casey said. "She said a few words at one of the meetings. She made me realize how third-world people feel when someone offers them a string of glass beads in exchange for, oh, say, a million square miles of their land and thinks it's a big favor." Casey walked on. "This is the place," she said suddenly. "The murderer strangled her here at the gate and pushed her body down the incline into the excavation."

Margaret looked down at deep tire tracks in the half-frozen mud, a few drifts of leftover snow, the flimsy fence with its gate open wide to allow the trucks to pass. This part of the block had a derelict look, as though the remaining buildings were merely waiting to be demolished, with boarded-up windows and lonely, bare stoops. Down the street a distance was a bodega with a couple of men standing about in the cold with brown bags holding cans of beer.

"If Sandy Krofft didn't come around the neighborhood often, what about Johnny Mascarpone?"

"Him." Casey almost laughed. "He tried hitting on me, but only once. He stops by the diner now and then, and I've seen him going into Larry's Bar."

"I'd like to see your photos sometime," Margaret said.

"What for?"

"You seem serious about your work. I'd like to see for myself."

"I've got to finish developing the pictures from last night. Rebecca is not happy I didn't get them done. But come in for a minute," Casey said.

She led Margaret to a three-story building like many of the others in the neighborhood and opened the gate, pausing to wave at a bearded man with three ferocious-looking dogs coming out of a house a few doors away.

A friendly neighborhood, Margaret thought, and wondered if the neighborliness would survive Carolyn Sue and Sandy Krofft.

Casey took her to the second floor and jiggled the lock. "Got to get this fixed. There."

The walls of a big, white, rugless room at the end of a short hallway were covered with eight by ten glossies: close-ups of faces of many races, long shots of people on the street, blow-ups of architectural details. Margaret walked past them slowly.

"That's Frances," Casey said, and pointed to a woman in profile shaking her finger at an unseen recipient of her words. Frances Rassell wore her gray hair short. She had a long, thin face. From the angle of the photo, it seemed that she wore a tight, smug smile.

Margaret moved on to another photo, a shot taken from a distance of a man sitting on the stoop of an old house with boarded-up windows. Margaret thought it was the man she'd seen sitting over coffee in the diner. There were many shots of the construction site—before and as work progressed.

"I like this one," Casey said. "Real life in Arcadia. That's Ernie Powers and his wife, Rita." A paunchy man and a bosomy woman with a look of discontent about her looked directly into the camera. "He sort of has a crush on me and has promised to fix my lock, not that there's much here to steal."

In fact, the apartment was furnished with two chairs, a table, and a rolled futon, with several enormous spider plants hanging from the ceiling in front of the windows.

"This is my darkroom." She opened a door off the hallway,

It wasn't much more than a large closet with a sink, three developing trays, and an enlarger, with an amber safe light above the door. Shelves of chemicals stood along one wall.

"It used to be a laundry room, I think," Casey said, "back in the days when this was a one-family house. That's it."

"You have quite an eye," Margaret said. She went back to the wall of photos to look again at a scene of a moderately busy shopping street. She was sure the man standing beside a telephone kiosk was John Mascarpone, talking to someone with his back to the camera. She thought that person could easily be Spiros.

"Thanks awfully for showing me your things," Margaret said. "I ought to be getting back to Manhattan."

Casey came down to the street with her. The man from the diner who Spiros had called Tommy was ambling in their direction. He paused uncertainly half a block away when he spotted Casey and Margaret.

"I say," Margaret said. "That fellow over there. I saw him at the diner earlier. He seems to be watching us."

"Tommy. He's always around, and he watches everything.

We chat now and then. He's kind of messed up, but okay. I think he wants to speak to me." Her tone indicated that it was between her and Tommy.

A few snowflakes were beginning to float down.

"Don't look for a cruising cab," Casey said. "The elevated station is a couple of blocks that way."

"Believe it or not, I have actually ridden the subway," Margaret said.

"Sure," Casey said. She did not sound convinced. "Midtown in twenty minutes. So near and yet so far. Look, I can't take any more time. . . ." She walked away abruptly toward Tommy.

There's a prickly one, Margaret thought.

The sky seemed low and loaded with snow as Margaret walked away. The houses seemed dingier, and a glimpse of the towers of Manhattan far away reminded her how close and how distant she was here from the expatriate life in the city she had made her own.

Margaret looked back. Casey's purple parka was visible through the thickening snow. She was walking away with the man called Tommy. They were head-to-head in conversation.

Chapter 9

Sandy Krofft phoned down from her office to her driver, who was waiting in the Lincoln town car outside the building that housed Castrocani Development.

"I will be leaving in ten minutes. We'll drop Mr. Mascarpone at his place and then go over to Queens. How are the roads?"

They didn't look bad yet to the driver, and he knew enough not to give Miss Krofft news she didn't want to hear until it was absolutely necessary. He also didn't choose to comment on the fact that she was taking a twenty-minute trip across the river a good two hours before this meeting was supposed to begin. Miss Krofft did not care to have anyone comment on her business.

Sandy tucked her long, blond hair under a big fur hat and put on a long, black coat that covered the tops of her low-heeled black boots. She checked her big, black shoulder bag and turned off the lights in her office.

The receptionist had already left. In fact, everyone had cleared out before five to beat the snow. Sandy stood at the back of the empty elevator car and watched the numbers of the floors click past.

Sandy wasn't sure about this Lady Margaret that Carolyn Sue Hoopes put such trust in. Sandy knew the type and resented it: social position, money, never required to work for a living. She couldn't be the totally empty-brained blue blood she appeared to be, but could she be a lot smarter than she seemed? Time would tell. Sandy intended to be standing at the back of the room, as anonymously as possible, when Margaret made her presentation. She hadn't mentioned that fact to Peter Wellington when she called him to confirm Margaret's appearance.

Johnny Mascarpone was waiting for her in the lobby. He'd been around the corner at the closest bar for his end-of-day cocktail with the men from nearby offices who used it as their midtown watering hole.

"You sure you don't want me to come with you?" Johnny asked. "You don't want me?"

Sandy pointedly ignored the hand that casually caressed her back, the look of simmering lust he liked to don, like one of his thousand-dollar suits, to impress women.

"Get serious, John," she said. She looked at him coldly. "You don't stand a chance with me. I tell you that how many times a day? Twice? Three times? I choose my men; I don't get chosen."

"I'm talking about this meeting."

"I can handle that. I don't like you around the neighborhood too much. I hope this Brit doesn't trigger some kind of disaster. At least we don't have to worry about Carolyn Sue. She's safely tucked away on that island. Let's go. The car's waiting. I have some business to attend to before the meeting."

The car pulled out into traffic with Sandy and Johnny in the luxurious leather backseat.

"Have you heard of cops who moonlight as drivers for the overprivileged?" she asked.

"Maybe some do, if the person is really rich or really famous. An old retired cop might like an easy job driving some fancy dame around the city. Hey," he added in a low voice, "how much does this guy of yours cost you really?"

"Never mind," Sandy said sharply. "It's a necessary business expense." She had nothing further to say to Johnny.

She never had much to say to him and suffered his presence in the office only because he was useful for certain chores she didn't care to undertake herself. He could put a little muscle into meetings with construction guys and city officials. She was too smart not to know that this was still a man's world, especially in the development business. She had the power, so she didn't mind playing the pretty office accessory when the occasion required.

"Be at the office early tomorrow," she said when the car pulled up to a new high-rise apartment building on Second Avenue near the Midtown Tunnel. "That so-called architect is coming at ten. You might as well be there to frown at him while I tell him how close his firm is to being fired off this job."

"I can never understand why they don't have everything designed before they start digging," Johnny said. "My father and uncles were in the construction business their whole lives, and they always knew what they were building before they started."

"They built two-car garages and sewers," Sandy said. "This is fast-track construction. Time is money, and we couldn't get it done if we didn't start the basements while the architects are still designing the walls."

"Yeah, sure," Johnny said. The car stopped in front of the tall apartment building. He didn't linger. "See ya." He waited until the town car pulled away into the falling snow and headed for the tunnel. Then he flagged down a passing cab.

Sandy leaned forward over the seat and said to the driver, "You can drop me in the neighborhood, and be ready to pick me up anytime. Park somewhere near the diner next to the construction site. I'll find you there when I shake loose."

Her driver nodded. He never figured out what business she had in Arcadia after dark. He would drop her off, and she'd walk off. Friends, she once said. Miss Krofft didn't have friends.

The snow let up some by the time they reached their destination a couple of blocks from Saint Lucy's Church. Sandy got out of the car quickly. She waited until the car moved silently off, leaving black tire tracks in the snow. Then she walked unnoticed along the neighborhood streets to her destination. No one was abroad at the supper hour. Sandy noticed the hand-lettered signs in the windows of the bodega and the newspaper store announcing the meeting and other signs taped on the streetlight posts. Much good it would do them.

She wasn't seeing the old houses and the slender bare trees, the lighted windows where behind the curtains young and old lives were sheltered from the snow and the rigors of life in New York. She saw an orderly and intricate complex of mixed-use buildings stretching for blocks: arcades, apartments, a hotel, shops, and offices. Neat, new, orderly, expensive.

Sandy Krofft smiled at the vision.

''Ah!'' The unshakable kingdom builder was shaken by the sight of a scrawny feral dog darting from under a parked car in front of her. It stopped and looked at her. The light from a streetlight reflected back orange from its wild eyes. Then it ran, low to the ground, and disappeared in the darkness.

Sandy shook off her momentary alarm. Too many troublemakers cowering in unexpected corners. She heard the roar of a motorcycle on the next block as she ascended the steps of a well-kept house and rang the doorbell.

Arthur Cramdell was nervous about speaking at the meeting tonight. He didn't like looking out at rows of faces who might be watching him with suspicion and even fear. But he'd do it. He'd kept silent long enough. He would make them understand what they'd been up against all along.

At first he didn't think he'd eat until after the meeting. Then he thought that if he waited, the grocery store would be closed. He couldn't face pizza from the neighborhood pizzeria or those bits of chicken and noodles at the Korean place that had been in the steam table for days and days. He decided to run over to the grocery store, pick up something, and then think about whether to eat now or later.

He met Rebecca Wellington on the street outside, just getting out of a taxi. Even though he didn't like her, he tried to be nice.

"You're home early," Arthur said. "Peter's home. He must have beat the snow by a couple of hours. I saw the lights when I got in. How's it going?"

"Lousy day," Rebecca said. "And I don't just mean the weather." She slammed the cab door and headed for the house. At least she wasn't going to linger.

As he walked through the snow, he mulled over the question of whether to congratulate Frances's murderer publicly.

"You made it home in time. Good." Peter Wellington kissed his wife. "I cut out early myself. Are you feeling okay?"

"I'm home in time because I knew you wanted me to be," she said. She knew he was pretending not to notice how tight her smile was. "I'm sorry I've been so bitchy lately, Peter. All this stress. You know."

"I understand. It'll be all right."

Inside she was not at peace, and it wouldn't be all right: Casey hadn't finished developing last night's photos as she'd promised. Some witch on Dianne's committee had called to complain about an item about the reception that had appeared in Poppy Dill's column—her name hadn't been mentioned.

She'd called Sandy Krofft today to see about the status of her proposal to represent the new building. With Frances Rassell's murder on top of everything else, Castrocani Development could use a good PR person. Although Sandy hadn't exactly turned her down, she hadn't been encouraging. Cold was more like it, although she'd been friendly enough the one time they'd met.

Rebecca needed a pickup badly.

"I'm so tired" was all she said to Peter.

"Sure, hon. I understand."

"You're *so* understanding. You're *so* calm and controlled." Peter didn't seem to notice the sarcasm in her voice.

"How did your meeting with this Harry Dodds go?" he asked.

"Dowd. He had to cancel. The weather." More likely a better offer, but Rebecca wasn't going to tell Peter that. "Look, let me run upstairs and microwave a delicious, nutritious something from the freezer. If nothing looks good, I'll go around the corner and pick up something. I can't face a neighborhood meeting on an empty stomach. I met Arthur going out as I came in. I almost asked him to dinner, but he's a bore."

"Arthur's okay," Peter said. "Pays his rent on time and no loud parties. He's signed up to speak tonight."

"Has he written a poem for the occasion? Sorry."

When Rebecca reached the top of the stairs, Peter called up after her. "Do we have any beer?"

She opened the refrigerator. "None in sight. There's wine. . . ."

"I feel like a beer," Peter said. "I'll pick some up at the bodega. Won't be five minutes."

She had a brilliant idea. "Peter, as long as you're going out, could you stop at Casey's and pick up my photos? She swore they'd be ready. . . . Peter, did you hear me?"

"Yes, sure."

Rebecca waited impatiently to hear the door slam. What was taking him so long?

"I'll be right back," she finally heard him say.

Simpler than she thought. She raced downstairs, threw on her coat and boots, and walked quickly through the snow in the opposite direction Peter had taken. This was only going to take a few minutes, and if Peter got back before she did, she'd have a head of lettuce in a supermarket shopping bag, a forgotten dinner item she'd gone out to buy.

With the snow falling, the street looked dreamy. Nobody had driven down it, so a smooth path of white lay between the cars parked at both curbs, slowly accumulating caps of white. One or two earnest householders had shoved the first inch of snow from the steps and the sidewalks in front of their houses, but mostly the sidewalks were as untouched as the street.

Tommy had grabbed some stew from Rita early, eaten it in the basement, and left the empty bowl upstairs in the kitchen. Ernie was at the kitchen table wolfing down the stew and sopping up the stuff with a big chunk of bread. He had glared at Tommy but couldn't leave it at that. He had to have words. "Where you going now? What you doing?" Rita had told him to shut up, but Tommy knew the signs. Maybe not tomorrow, but the next day or next week, Ernie would start asking whether he was going to find a place of his own. Well, okay. Maybe now he could tell Ernie off and leave. Maybe there was money coming his way. Money for silence.

Tommy pulled up his collar and trudged through the snow. His shoes were not so good; he could feel the dampness through the shabby leather.

He wondered if he'd said too much to too many people. He hadn't mentioned any names, but maybe one of the guys at Larry's Bar had repeated something he'd said and it had gotten back to somebody. It couldn't have been the lawyer, because Tommy hadn't really told him anything. He'd just said a friend of his had maybe seen a crime being committed, and what would happen if he didn't go to the police?

Peter Wellington had asked where and who and when, and did it have something to do with drugs?

Tommy had been cagey. "In the neighborhood, last week. It was just some guy. Not drugs. A little . . . little rough stuff somebody pulled . . ."

Had the lawyer noticed he was nervous? Tommy didn't think so, but in the end, he hadn't been much help. "A duty to inform the police, could this friend of his identity the perpetrator, blah, blah, blah." And some stuff about not being really up on the criminal side of the law, being a tax lawyer and all that.

Tommy had told Casey only a little more this afternoon. He'd mentioned Frances. Maybe that had been a mistake. He'd mentioned the note without saying exactly what was in it.

Tommy huddled deeper into his coat and walked on through the falling snow toward the house where Gracie Fogel had lived back in those good days when he didn't have any worries. The note had been handed to him this afternoon by a neighborhood kid who found him killing time in the shelter of the elevator after Spiros threw him out of the diner. All it said was: Be at the old houses across from the construction site. Six o'clock. It will be financially rewarding.

"Where'dya get this?" he'd asked the kid, who shrugged. One of the usual idiots these mothers were raising. Couldn't talk.

"You stupid, kid? Or don't you want to tell me?"

"The Korean. Said somebody gave it to him to find somebody to give it to you. Gave me five bucks to do it." The kid looked put out about the amount. It would have seemed like a fortune when Tommy was that age. Kids.

So that was it. He knew it wouldn't do him any good to try to find out anything from the Korean. Wouldn't tell him if he knew, and besides, the same person never seemed to be at the cash register for two hours running.

But Tommy had a plan. He'd stay in the shadows, see who showed up. He wondered if Frances's murderer would be nuts enough to come in person. Maybe somebody else would come with the payoff. He didn't care. He was ready to swear to anybody that he didn't see who did it. He'd take the money and go West. He'd been in San Diego years ago when he was in the service. Nice town. He'd like to see it again. No snow.

He heard a loud roar as someone gunned a badly tuned car. He looked around. Nothing to see but that creepy guy who lived upstairs above the lawyer. He was walking with his head down, carrying a supermarket shopping bag. He'd once overheard Frances telling Anita, the waitress at the diner, that the guy was crazy and everybody knew he was responsible for the rotten eggs. Tommy kept walking, keeping close to the buildings so he wouldn't be noticed. He heard the squeal of skidding tires and looked back over his shoulder.

"Oh, jeez, what else?" was all he could think. A dilapidated van raced down the street and just missed the guy with the shopping bag as he was crossing. The guy sprawled on the road, and his shopping bag went flying. The van stopped, skidding again on the slick, snow-covered road. For a minute Tommy was certain the driver was backing up to have another try at the guy who was down.

Then an enraged Arthur Cramdell scrambled to his feet and reached the sidewalk. He shook his fist and yelled, "Assassin!" as the van sped away.

Tommy sighed. Two murders in one week would be more than he could take. He'd seen a lot of people die, but far away on the other side of the world. Not in his own neighborhood.

He walked on cautiously. He was close to the rendezvous spot now. He looked around and saw no one. A car was double-parked up the block with its engine running, so he drew back into the shadows until it drove away. Nice car, too nice for this neighborhood.

When the coast was clear, Tommy quickly crossed the street, and in a second he had disappeared into the dark doorway above the stoop of Gracie's old house.

Chapter 10

By the time De Vere arrived uptown at Margaret's apartment building to take her across to Queens, the snow was falling steadily.

"I want to appear presentable, serious, and not gaudy," Margaret said. She had indeed left her mink at home.

"Very presentable," De Vere said. "Where is this place?"

Margaret read off the address, a mysterious series of numbers attached to a numbered street. De Vere didn't seem troubled at all.

"There was a rowdy Irish bar not far from there, a place called Larry's," he said. "I used to hang out there in my social days."

De Vere seldom talked about his past. She'd known for a long time that he'd once been married, but he never said a negative word about his ex-wife, except to note that being married to a policeman was not the most stress-free life for a woman. She'd come to terms with the idea that De Vere wasn't looking for anything more substantial than the relationship they now enjoyed. Indeed, she doubted that she would be better off in different circumstances. The conventional forms of love and marriage in New York were for the impetuous young, the unbalanced, or the sinfully rich. She was none of the above.

78

As they headed for the on ramp toward the upper level of the Fifty-ninth Street Bridge, she wondered if the wife whose name she did not know had hung out with De Vere and his buddies in the cozy, dark-paneled Queens pub she imagined. Tough old bartender, big wooden bar, and jaunty, wisecracking waitresses.

"Fasten your seat belt," he said. "I'd hate to lose you on an icy side street in Queens."

"That's nice," she said absently. "I spoke to Carolyn Sue again this morning. She was lounging on her patio with a background of steel drums."

"I've never been to the Caribbean," De Vere said.

"Carolyn Sue is paying me so much to do her dirty work," Margaret said, "we could afford a long weekend."

He didn't say anything, but at least he didn't say no.

"This is it" was what he said.

Saint Lucy's Church was a dark pile of red brick with a modest steeple. Faint illumination from within shone through a series of semigothic stained-glass windows. It looked to be a product of the affluent middle-class era of Arcadia around the turn of the century. The snow-covered statue of Saint Lucy in front of the church looked chilly and forlorn, but appropriately blind to the arrival of Lady Margaret and De Vere.

Margaret hesitated at the door of Saint Lucy's parish hall. Now that the time had come to speak, Margaret felt a bit nervous. De Vere touched her arm and muttered, "Bravely into the fray."

Margaret took a deep breath and opened the door, to be met by a blast of hot, damp air, the curious eyes of a packed room, and two men standing side by side. One was a very young priest with screen-idol good looks and a worried expression and the other a thirtyish man with round wire glasses and combed-back blondish hair. He was wearing a dark pinstriped suit with a vest and looked like nothing other than an earnest young lawyer.

"Lady Margaret?" the priest said. "I'm Father Steve. I was asked to watch for you, and . . ."

"Peter Wellington," the other man said. He didn't exactly elbow the priest out of the way, but it was clear he thought of himself as the one in charge. "Sandy Krofft's office telephoned to say you'd be representing Castrocani Development tonight."

"How nice of you to welcome me, Father Steve," Margaret said, before turning her attention to Peter Wellington. "I prefer to think I'm representing Mrs. Benton Hoopes, Mr. Wellington, rather than a big corporation. Let me introduce Mr. De Vere."

Both the priest and Peter surveyed De Vere as though they didn't quite know what to make of this unlikely person accompanying the aristocratic Lady Margaret. As usual, De Vere was dressed in pressed jeans, with a dark blue crewneck sweater, and a well-worn but distinguished sheepskin jacket. His low boots were polished to a shine and looked capable of warding off any degree of slush, salt, or other hazards of winter walking in the city.

"We have quite a full house," Father Steve said nervously.

Margaret looked over the room. The folding chairs set in rows were filled with people. Some looked curiously at her over their shoulders. Many whispered with their heads together, perhaps discussing the visitor from the other side of the water. The East River could seem a formidable barrier dividing two worlds.

"I should tell you," Father Steve said, "that I . . . Saint Lucy's . . . try to keep from taking a specific position. We make our space available to the community. Well, um . . . Mr. Wellington will see to you and Mr. De Vere." He looked relieved to have done his part in introducing her to a bucket of worms. "Mrs. Rassell was a member of our parish," he said suddenly. "She'll be buried from here. I didn't know her well. Some of the older ladies regretted the retirement of Father O'Malley."

The priest wandered away, speaking a word or two to some of the seated attendees. Then he took the opportunity to slip out through a side door, perhaps to say a prayer that his parish hall would survive the meeting.

Peter Wellington said, "Father Steve arrived after the first stages of protest. He's not sure if he should be on one side or the other. Father O'Malley was opposed to the new building because he didn't like to see changes in the old neighborhood."

"Everything changes," Margaret said. "But surely he has taken a position on the murder."

Peter was briefly flustered. "What? Oh, yes. A terrible tragedy. I was very fond of Frances. The neighborhood is shattered."

"Indeed," Margaret said. "And are you fond of this building?"

"I try to see both sides. Economically, it's probably a good idea, but I hate to see people steamrollered. I try to be . . . um . . . fair. It's all quite legal, but . . ." He straightened his navy blue tie with a red stripe. "Now, about the meeting. The way things have been arranged, a few people have signed up to speak one more time. Grievances about alleged promises not kept, complaints about the construction. We'll get them out of the way, and then you can say whatever you'd like and leave."

"I'd be quite happy to answer questions," Margaret said, "if I have the answers."

"No, no. You're not to take any questions. They'll be grateful for what the company is giving to them. You and your . . . friend can sit off to the side before you address them."

"That sounds fine," Margaret said. "What promises?" She wondered exactly how much Peter Wellington knew about what Carolyn Sue was giving to the people of Arcadia.

"People took some things that were said too literally," Peter said. "Renovations of existing structures and the like."

"How *lovely* to see you again!"

Margaret was face-to-face with Rebecca Wellington, all tarted up in a designer suit and expensive boots, with a bold pink- and green-plaid coat slung over her shoulders. Margaret was sure she had seen it in the pages of *Vogue*.

"I had *no* idea you'd be here. Peter, darling, you didn't

tell me that Lady Margaret Priam would be here.'' Rebecca was frantically animated, rather more than the occasion of running into Lady Margaret Priam demanded. ''Lady Margaret and I met at Dianne Stark's charity committee reception the other night. Remember, I told you?'' Peter Wellington looked blank as Rebecca turned her big, bright public relations smile on Margaret again. ''Whatever brings you here?''

''She's representing Mrs. Hoopes,'' Peter said. ''Darling, why don't you . . .''

''Carolyn Sue! How divine! What a lovely woman. So . . . So . . .''

''Rich,'' De Vere said helpfully. Rebecca took him in briefly and did not seem impressed.

''And I had no idea I'd be meeting you again in this particular setting,'' Margaret said.

''We have a quaint little house just down the road—our cottage in the midst of the urban sprawl. We're doing a total remodel. A lot of work, but it will be adorable. Beautiful old wood floors and tin ceilings and masses of roses in the garden come spring.'' She made it sound as though it had sprung full-blown from a Martha Stewart dream, scented with rose petal potpourri and Rigaud candles, crammed to the attics with Laura Ashley prints and Ralph Lauren knickknacks, with the odd spinning wheel and King Charles spaniel at the hearthside to round out the picture. ''I was just saying to Harry Dowd the other day that it's such a special thing to have a sweet little house practically in the middle of the city that you can mold to your tastes. I do admire Harry's taste.''

''Harry does have painfully exquisite taste,'' Margaret said, remembering the magnificent clutter of antique snuffboxes, silver spoons, puppets, china dogs, buttons, and shoe buckles crammed into his too-precious house in the Hamptons. She looked over Rebecca's shoulder and saw Casey Teale come through the door with her camera ready for a telling human interest shot. Casey nodded once in her direction but hung back. She looked tired and preoccupied.

''There's the photographer who was with you the other night.'' Margaret interrupted Rebecca's chatter, which was continuing unchecked. De Vere took the opportunity to abandon her and stroll around the perimeter of the room. To her eyes, he looked very policemanlike, checking out the usual suspects, but no one paid him any heed. He had a gift for taking on the coloration of his environment.

"Casey? She's from the neighborhood and *forever* snapping pictures of the buildings and the people around here. They don't seem to mind. I can't say I like her arty things. . . ."

Margaret caught herself before she disagreed. She was supposed to be a total stranger in the neighborhood.

Finally Peter said, "Rebecca, my love, why don't you run along to your seat while I brief Lady Margaret?"

Rebecca pouted. "I wanted Casey to get a photo of Margaret and me together. It's the least she can do after wrecking my day by not having last night's photos ready. I tell you, Margaret, these free-lancers . . ." Rebecca had the audacity to link arms with Margaret, who shuddered inwardly. She did not care for the presumption of intimacy when it was an obvious attempt to cozy up for selfish ends.

"Is a photo really necessary, Mrs. Wellington?" Margaret asked, and knew it was too late. Peter had gone to fetch Casey.

"A bit of our little neighborhood's history," Rebecca said, too gaily for the circumstances. "That's what everyone seems to be into nowadays."

"Useful, too, I imagine," Margaret murmured, "should Sandy Krofft require a glamour shot for public relations purposes."

Rebecca became defensive. "I have nothing to do with Sandy Krofft. My husband knows her better than I do."

"Hello again," Casey said as Peter steered her to them. She continued to watch the door out of the corner of her eye, even as she posed Margaret and Rebecca.

"Casey, dear, you *will* have my photos tomorrow," Rebecca stated, trying to sound sweet but coming off as simply annoyed. "Peter tramped all the way to your house for them and didn't get an answer to his ring."

"I was in the darkroom," Casey said shortly.

A few latecomers straggled in, shaking the snow off their coats and stamping their feet. The audience was restless.

"Let's get on with this," Peter said. He sounded impatient. "I am chairing the meeting. To keep things in order, I'm going to cut people off after five minutes."

"Then I'll just join my . . . my driver off to the side," Margaret said, "and compose myself."

Casey said, "Could I speak to you before you leave? I need . . ." She stopped and glanced at Rebecca.

"Certainly," Margaret said quickly. "Right after I speak my piece." Rebecca glared at the competition for Margaret's attention, then flounced off to her seat. "Is anything wrong?"

"No," Casey said slowly. "It's probably nothing."

De Vere had placed two chairs against the wall, away from the rows of seats but not far from the front. Thankfully, Margaret was not in the audience's line of sight.

"How do you read the temper of the mob?" she asked.

"Restless, some angry comments," De Vere said. "A few loud complainers. Some staunch defenders of progress, as they call it. It sounds like every neighborhood meeting I've ever been to. Carolyn Sue's crumbs aren't going to drive away the bad feelings."

"Are you worried about my reception?"

"We're not talking about people whipped up into a frenzy and out for blood, so I don't think they're looking for your head to post on a spike at the crossroads."

"I and my class thank you so much for your support," Margaret said, and he grinned at her.

"I'll save you from the tumbrils," he said. "This time."

The buzz ceased as Peter Wellington took his place facing the crowd. He looked surprisingly sharp and assured.

The room in the parish hall wasn't a true auditorium. There was a sort of dais at one end for speakers, but otherwise it was a functional, all-purpose room with children's drawings tacked on a bulletin board and some folding tables stacked along the wall, ready for a rummage sale or potluck supper.

"Quiet, please," Peter said. "We'll get right to business.

Father Steve . . ." He looked around. The priest was back, standing at the sidelines. "Father Steve has offered to say a few words in memory of our unfortunate neighbor, Frances Rassell."

There was a rising murmur in the audience. Somebody said, "*Murdered* neighbor," and was shushed by those seated around him.

Father Steve's words were few, and correct, in that they acknowledged Frances's life and death without extolling her insincerely—and no mention was made of her connection with the building protests or why anyone would want to kill her.

Most people, Margaret noted, bowed their heads, but one or two watched the priest almost defiantly. One was a burly man in work clothes, the other a neatly dressed, unsmiling young man with fair features who looked straight ahead. Casey moved restlessly along the back of the room, looking at the door from time to time. Margaret wondered who was late, whom she was expecting.

"Mmm." De Vere startled her. She looked in the same direction and saw that a man had opened the door and was peering into the room. For a moment, she saw his face clearly. Then he stepped back, and the door closed on him.

At the priest's "amen," she whispered, "Sam?"

"I thought I recognized the man who started to come in," De Vere said, as Peter Wellington reminded those who had signed up to speak how much time they were allotted.

"How curious," Margaret said. "I did recognize him. His name is Spiros. He owns a diner in the neighborhood."

"I won't ask how you know that," he said. "I remember him from my days in and around Queens."

Peter Wellington gave way to the first speaker, a slight, nervous man with a heavy Spanish accent. His short statement was a list of complaints: the noisy trucks, his rising rent, a wall in his apartment already cracked from one of the early dynamite blasts. What had happened to the renovations that had been promised for his building? He asked questions, but he did not sound much in hope of answers. His frustration drew applause.

He was followed by others: a wild-haired young woman who seemed to espouse a number of radical positions, few of them clearly related to the matter at hand. She praised Frances Rassell for her activism in opposing the greedy forces of big business. More applause. A couple of men detailed facts and statistics about environmental impact, traffic patterns, pressure on public services. An elderly woman spoke about ill-defined hardships and the "undesirable element" the building was bringing in. Then a no-nonsense black woman made it clear she didn't like the influx of hookers and drug dealers around the neighborhood since the building started going up. She demanded to know why something wasn't being done about the vandals who threw rotten eggs at her door and her neighbors'. A bearded man with a slight accent spoke about the declining quality of life and how crass materialism was stifling the creative spirit, until Peter Wellington reminded him that his time was up.

De Vere was becoming bored.

"It won't take much longer, surely," Margaret said.

De Vere grimaced. "They have no coherence, no clout, not even the press to bolster them. And all of this is much too late to make any difference."

The burly man in work clothes stood up at his place. "I ain't signed up to speak, but let me say just one thing. You all know me, Ernie Powers, and you know I believe in plain speaking."

"Sit down, Ernie," someone said from the back. "It's not your turn."

Ernie ignored the interruption. "All I'm saying is, what harm can one building do? What is it? Twenty stories tall? No big thing. This neighborhood was a dump when I was a kid, and it still is. Maybe this will make a difference."

"Mr. Powers," Peter Wellington said, "your point is well taken, and if there's time at the end, we'll give you your chance to speak, but this time is reserved for . . ." He made a point of looking over his list. "Arthur Cramdell."

The nice-looking young man who had no prayer for Frances Rassell took the stage. "I don't know many of you, because I only moved here a few months ago. My name is Arthur Cramdell."

"We know about you, fella," someone said. Arthur Cramdell fixed his gaze on the back of the hall and continued.

"This building may end up being a good thing for the neighborhood or a bad thing, but if you have any sense, you know there's nothing you can do about it. It's going to happen." He took a deep breath. "What you should know is that all along you've been lied to by people you think are your friends. That includes Frances Rassell, among others."

"Now just a minute!" Frances Rassell's daughter, Alice, was dressed in black as befitted a relative of the deceased, but she was less bereaved than angry. "Ma said you couldn't be trusted. You're trying to get even now that she's dead."

"You're going to say that I am speaking out of vindictiveness because Frances spread rumors about me." Arthur was not to be stopped. "Like all rumors, they had a little truth to them. I was hospitalized once for a mental breakdown, but that's all in the past. I am not a convicted criminal; I am not a dangerous person." Another deep breath, and Arthur plunged ahead. The audience was leaning forward intently. "Frances Rassell was the dangerous person. She was a friend of the developers, not a friend of the neighborhood. She was being paid off right up to the day she died. And she wasn't the only one. There are people around who won't stop at anything. Just tonight I was almost run down by a van. There are people who don't care about any of us—they want us out of this neighborhood, so they can profit."

Margaret thought his words had the ring of paranoia. His listeners shifted uneasily. Ernie Powers was scowling. The large woman beside him shook her head vigorously. Alice sat stony-faced, with her arms folded.

"Arthur," Peter said warningly. "Don't you think . . ."

Arthur ignored him. "I'm glad Mr. Powers spoke up just now, because he's absolutely wrong. This isn't about just one twenty-story building. It's about twenty buildings, fifty. I don't know. There's a plan that will wipe Arcadia off the map and replace it with a 'planned community.' Do you like the sound of that? There's a war beginning right here in Arcadia, and you people are going to be the casualties . . . and . . . and . . . That's all I have to say.'' Arthur walked to his seat, picked up his coat, and left the hall, while his audience silently watched him go.

"What was *that* all about?" Margaret whispered. "He sounded slightly hysterical."

De Vere shrugged. "Part getting even, part truth, maybe. I wonder if my colleagues have checked him out. He did seem a little unbalanced."

Peter Wellington took center stage. "Mr. Cramdell was the last person signed up to speak. . . ."

"I have something to say." Alice was on her feet. "You sit down, Ernie."

Margaret hoped the woman wasn't going to launch into an impassioned plea for justice.

"I'm not going to sit here and hear my poor, dear mother slandered by that . . . that . . ."

"Go back to Long Island, Alice," Ernie said loudly.

Alice ignored him, and Peter let her continue. "She was a good, hardworking woman, and she was shamefully murdered not three blocks from here. I'd like to meet the person who did it face-to-face. But right now, I'd like to know what we're going to get from this company that took away my mother from me and her little grandchildren." Alice appeared to wipe away a tear.

There were loud murmurs now, and people were looking over at Margaret. Peter Wellington raised a finger in Margaret's direction.

She took a single sheet of paper from her bag and breathed deeply. "Wish me luck," she said. De Vere patted her hand.

"Lady Margaret Priam is representing Mrs. Benton Hoopes," Peter said. "Mrs. Hoopes is the principal owner of Castrocani Development and is unfortunately out of the country, so she cannot speak to you herself."

"Coward," Margaret thought she heard someone mutter as she took center stage.

"Um, yes. Hullo," Margaret said to the rows of faces before her. "My name . . . that is, I am Margaret Priam. . . ."

Was her English accent too awful for the occasion? What did they think of this foreigner in their midst? She looked at her paper and then at the back of the room, hoping to take strength and inspiration from the large portrait of Pope John Paul on the far wall of Saint Lucy's parish hall. What she got for her trouble was a moment of confusion, as she thought she recognized Sandy Krofft in a plain coat and a close-fitting fur hat get up from a chair at the back and slip away quietly.

"Mrs. Hoopes is greatly troubled that her project has caused so much . . . so much bad feeling," Margaret said. "However, there is no truth in the rumor that her company had something to do with the death of Mrs. Rassell."

She suddenly remembered what Arthur Cramdell had said: "Like all rumors . . . a little truth . . ."

She plunged bravely on with her speech. "There is no way that the process that has been set in motion can be reversed, but Mrs. Hoopes believes you will be pleased to learn that she has made these provisions for you."

Then Margaret lost her audience. From somewhere not far away, the sound of a dull, deep explosion reached the room, and the floor throbbed gently beneath the rows of folding chairs.

Chapter 11

De Vere was the first to reach the door. Margaret saw him raise his hand in her direction. She imagined that he was telling her to wait here. Then he disappeared. The neighborhood people were slower to react. They stood about confused, milled in groups, and gabbled to one another. Peter Wellington stepped up on the platform next to Margaret.

"Order, order," he said, but no order ensued. Then people started to advance toward the door, and the sound level rose. "Ladies and gentlemen . . ." Peter was ignored as the crowd headed to the exit, and the room emptied, leaving only Margaret and the Wellingtons. Faint sirens could be heard in the streets outside the parish hall.

"This neighborhood is impossible!" Rebecca said. "Any little thing sets them off."

"Ought we to check on what's happened?" Margaret said. "It sounded like an explosion."

"It couldn't have been blasting at the site," Peter said. "They've only just started that, and they don't do it at night."

"I really ought to find out. . . ." Margaret said, and was ready to plunge out into the cold night, despite De Vere's indication that he wanted her to stay put. She fetched her coat to venture forth but was stopped at the door by Rebecca.

"Do come to brunch on Sunday," Rebecca said. "I'm

having some lovely people in. Friends from the city. One or two of the *nicer* neighborhood people . . .''

"Rebecca," Peter said, "not now, for God's sake." He appeared to find Rebecca's social arrangement as incongruous under the circumstances as Margaret did.

Margaret said as she managed to edge away out the door, "I'll have to check my engagements. You're in the book? I'll ring you." She escaped Rebecca, only to barely avoid a collision with Father Steve. "Ooops, sorry, Father. Lovely to meet you. I'm sorry I didn't have a chance . . . There seems to be trouble outside. . . .''

"Very troubling. I wonder. . . . Some of these old houses still have gas fixtures from the days when they used gas for lighting." He seemed reluctant to let her pass. "When I was given this parish, I was told that it was a quiet little neighborhood. I'd been hoping for a parish in real need of spiritual guidance. I wanted to help the poor and the disadvantaged. . . .''

"How . . . admirable," Margaret said. The sirens were growing louder. She didn't want to miss what was happening. "I really ought to be going." She looked over her shoulder, unwilling to be trapped again by the Wellingtons.

"Ah, yes. Since the meeting is over, I'll go back in and see about closing up." He grinned. "And permit you to escape into the night."

"Thank you so much," she said. The sound of the sirens was bouncing off the walls of the buildings on the street. "Mrs. Hoopes has promised a seniors center and a park," she added hastily. "Someone will let you know."

Father Steve called after her, "Frances Rassell's death. It must have been something personal. I can't see it any other way. Very troubling."

Margaret headed toward a glowing scene: a fire being extinguished by an array of fire equipment, many spotlights and flashing red lights from police cars and emergency vehicles. Up ahead she could see Spiros's diner and beyond it a crowd of the curious straining to get a better look. Red Con Edison emergency trucks were converging. Margaret had the impression that a large gap now existed where a building she'd seen earlier that day had once stood. She glimpsed De Vere conferring with a uniformed policeman and some men in plainclothes.

She could see Casey shooting pictures of her neighbors and the eerily lighted scene. The snow had stopped, leaving a couple of slippery inches underfoot.

A van with the logo of a local television station pulled up, and from it emerged a finely coiffed young woman with a microphone and a cameraman balancing a camera on his shoulder. Margaret recognized the reporter as someone with a too-cute name who reported from the scene on the local eleven o'clock television news. The reporter tried to move in on De Vere and his plainclothes colleagues. A couple of uniformed police officers put her off. Undeterred by losing that interview, the reporter started for the crowd of onlookers, microphone at the ready.

Margaret intercepted her. "Sorry to trouble you while you're working."

The young woman turned at the sound of the English voice. "Do you know something about this? Anybody hurt?" She put the mike in Margaret's face and signaled the cameraman.

"No. I mean," Margaret added quickly, "I don't really know. I was in the neighborhood when it happened. You arrived on the scene rather quickly."

The reporter lowered the mike, disappointed. No exclusive eyewitness interview here. "My assignment editor sent me out," she said. "Didn't say what it was. He said there'd been problems here, and there was some kind of trouble tonight."

"When was that? When were you sent out?"

The reporter was wary. "Half an hour ago, maybe? Look, I have to get going." Then she was gone. It did appear that the competition, both television and the press, was beginning to assemble. Someone had gone to some trouble to be sure that the explosion in Arcadia was well covered by the news media.

Suddenly Margaret's attention was drawn to a big, sleek car idling across the way. The window in the backseat was rolled down, and she caught a glimpse of a pale face topped by a close-fitting fur hat. The person appeared to be speaking on a cellular phone while observing the street. Margaret edged through the onlookers, trying to stay inconspicuous. She was thankful that no one seemed to recall that she was the representative of the hated developer—at least no one noticed her except an unknown person who collected a handful of the new-fallen snow, shaped it into a small, hard ball, and propelled it accurately and with some force into the small of her back.

Margaret stumbled and gasped as it hit her, but when she looked around, no one was looking at her; no one was slinking away with a guilty expression. She turned her attention again to the dark car. The window rose with electronic smoothness, and the smoked glass hid the passenger.

I wonder, Margaret thought, why Sandy Krofft is lurking around Arcadia after all.

Rebecca Wellington caught up with Margaret.

"Really! What now?" Rebecca said. She seemed agitated that these noisy and possibly dangerous events were disturbing her personal space. A moment later, Peter joined them. He put a protective arm around Rebecca. This did not appear to calm her.

"It doesn't look serious," Peter said, "unless it was a gas explosion. Maybe some amateur was making bombs."

"Is Arcadia a hotbed of amateur bomb makers, then?" Margaret was curious.

"No, no. You misunderstood," Peter said quickly. "That row of houses was scheduled to be demolished soon, in any case. Owned by Castrocani."

"I see," Margaret said. "A part of the scare tactics people have been talking about, a bid for more media attention? The television people were here promptly."

"I think not," Peter said. "All that business has been grossly overstated. You know what people are like when they gossip."

"Indeed I do," Margaret said.

"I want to go home," Rebecca said. "I've had just about enough for today."

"In a minute, hon. I want to find out something from Casey." Peter walked away. Rebecca's displeasure was mounting. She stamped her feet, either from the cold or pure annoyance, and pulled the pink- and green-plaid coat closer around her.

"Damn Frances," Rebecca said. "This is all her fault. She's haunting me. She's tried to cause me trouble since we bought that house. Outsiders, she called us. Peter pretended she was okay, but she was a nobody who paid too much attention to other people's business. Oh, do come *on*, Peter." She stood on tiptoe to look over the crowd. "What is he doing now? There's Casey. . . ."

Margaret looked around and saw Peter Wellington coming back from a different direction, from where the black car that sheltered Sandy Krofft was moving off into the night.

"Watch it, lady." Margaret had backed into the big man who'd spoken earlier at the meeting.

"So sorry," Margaret said. Rebecca had discovered Peter and was waving to him impatiently.

"Ah, you." Ernie Powers eyed her somewhat lecherously. "You some kind of spy for the builders?"

"Not I," Margaret said.

"Ernie!" A disheveled woman of ample proportions, who'd been at the meeting with Ernie, shoved her way toward them. "Ernie, did you hear?" She dabbed at her eyes with a tattered tissue. Her voice rose, and a great tear escaped the tissue and rolled down her cheek. "He . . . They . . ."

"Whatddaya want now, Rita?"

"They just found Tommy in there. Tommy's dead." Policemen in large numbers were converging on the remains of the building.

Ernie hesitated. "No kidding? Dead?" He seemed neither shocked nor surprised, merely interested. "You sure?" She nodded, on the brink of an attack of sobs. "Quit blubbering, Rita. He was a pest. So what if he got blown up."

"Ernie, he was family." Rita's lip was aquiver, and tears were beginning to well up again.

Peter Wellington said, "I heard, Mrs. Powers. It's too bad."

Rebecca seemed to have no words of condolence for Rita. In fact, by her expression, she seemed to agree with Ernie.

"Let's go," Ernie said, suddenly uncomfortable with the band of listeners. "There's that priest you like so much."

Rita put her hand to her heaving bosom. "At least poor Tommy will have last rites." As Ernie hustled Rita away into the darkness, Margaret saw Father Steve, coatless and wearing a narrow purple ecclesiastical stole around his neck, hurrying toward an ambulance that had backed up near the demolished building.

So, Margaret thought, someone had been killed by the explosion, and someone had summoned the priest. Then she shook her head: Tommy? Casey's friend? Margaret looked around to find Casey but could not see her in the crowd.

"Nothing more to see," Peter said. "Let's go home, hon. Everything's okay now. We'll hear all about it tomorrow."

It was a relief to see Rebecca and Peter depart for their urban oasis to warm themselves before the burning logs with hot toddies in their hands and snuggly cashmere blankets over their knees. At least, that is how Margaret chose to picture the Wellingtons at home in mid-February.

Margaret looked around for De Vere, but he was momentarily lost to view. Then she saw Casey standing alone, as close to the cordoned-off site as she was allowed, but she wasn't taking photos. She was staring at the pile of rubble. Only the well-worn stoop had survived.

"Casey," Margaret said. Casey had a remote look on her face. "The man who was killed . . ."

Casey turned to her. "Tommy Falco. After the fire was out, they found him. You saw him this afternoon."

"Yes. You said he hung around the neighborhood. He must have chosen the wrong place at the worst possible time."

Casey shook her head. "He didn't die in the explosion," she said. "He was killed before it happened."

"How do you know that?"

"I heard the police say he was found at the bottom of the steps. Strangled with a wire. Some debris from the explosion fell on him after he was dead. That's what they're saying." Casey looked troubled. "Tommy told me something this afternoon. He told me he'd seen Frances Rassell's murder."

"A murdered witness to a murder? Did you tell the police?" Margaret asked. "Wait. You said 'the murder.' Did he see the person who did it? Recognize him?"

"He said he didn't know who, but he told me . . ." Casey looked over her shoulder. The people who remained at the scene were still too interested in watching the comings and goings of police and firemen to pay attention to a conversation between the two women. "He said he was meeting someone tonight who was going to pay him to go away, to keep quiet about the murder. I told him not to go, but why would he listen to me? He was planning to come to the meeting afterward. I should have stopped him from going, and now he's dead."

"It's not your fault," Margaret said. "How did someone know what he'd seen? Who did he tell other than you?"

Casey made a face. "He confessed he talked big at Larry's Bar, where a lot of neighborhood guys hang out. They're as bad a bunch of gossips as those society ladies on East End Avenue."

"You must tell the police," Margaret said. "And you must be careful. If the person who killed your friend and possibly Mrs. Rassell thinks you know something . . ."

"I'll be all right," Casey said.

"There's Sam De Vere, who came with me tonight," Margaret said. She waved to catch his attention. "He's with the police, and he's easy to talk to. . . ." She looked around, but Casey had already walked away. Margaret saw her talking with a forlorn-looking Arthur Cramdell. Then another man joined them, and they left together.

"Come this way," a man's voice said. A strong and inescapable hand gripped Margaret's upper arm, and she was propelled from where she stood.

"I'd rather not," Margaret said, and tried to pull away while peering over her shoulder. The man who held her was a stranger to her.

"Don't give me an argument, lady," he said. "I'm not goin' to hurt you."

Margaret struggled a bit, if only to turn about to locate De Vere, but he was no longer in sight.

"I shall scream," she said, even as she was being hustled along away from the crowd and down a street lined with low, windowless brick buildings. They appeared to be warehouses with wide doorways suitable for trucks, although they were now tightly shuttered with corrugated steel security doors. She had the vague sense that people were standing in the shadows of recessed doorways.

She could see the Manhattan skyline in the distance. All those lights meant spacious, warm apartments filled with gracious people, cramped studios filled with eager youth driven to make their mark on the city, elegant restaurants with attentive waiters, Broadway theaters bursting with applause. . . .

Margaret stopped abruptly and screamed.

"Jeez," the man said as he put a leather glove across her mouth. "What did you want to go and do that for?" He cautiously removed his hand. "There's nobody around who's going to hear you."

Margaret glared at him. He was still holding her arm. She hated the sense of being powerless. "I did it because I don't like being abducted." She hoped she sounded as angry as she felt.

"I'm not abducting you. Somebody wants to see you." He stopped in front of a one-story yellowish brick building. A small sign on the side of the building said ACME IMPORT/ EXPORT. He pressed a bell beside a narrow barred door, and someone could be heard unbolting numerous locks.

"If anything happens to me," Margaret said, "I'll have

you know that I was here tonight with a member of the New York City police. He will be deeply concerned.''

"Just shut up, lady. I don't care if you were here with the mayor. This is just a friendly little visit."

A muscular youth opened the door to admit them and stood aside to let them pass. He looked like an average New York punk but tended toward the more extreme end of current fashion in hair and decoration. Four earrings in one ear and a ponytail, Margaret noticed. He slumped back on the chair beside the door and picked up a well-thumbed biker's magazine.

"Straight ahead," her abductor said. He pushed her through another door into a dimly lighted room furnished as a fairly comfortable office with a large desk on which were several telephones. There were lots of filing cabinets and a couple of monstrous rubber plants with dusty leaves.

"So," Spiros said from his seat behind the desk. "What's your game?"

"So," Margaret said, and sat down in a chair facing him, "what's yours?"

Chapter 12

"*Coffee?*" *Spiros* asked instead of answering. "Maybe a little glass of Metaxa, five star, very nice? It's cold out there. You like ouzo?"

"Nothing, thank you," Margaret said as coldly as she dared, not knowing what was to come next. "I really can't stay. My escort will be frantic."

Spiros leaned back in his chair and frowned. "Imagine my surprise to see you at the meeting tonight. And your friend." He shook his head. "A nice young lady comes into my diner in the afternoon, and by nighttime she's the agent for a big real estate developer. She's with a cop I remember from years ago. Still a cop, is he? I don't like surprises. Or spies."

"Oh, please. This whole bloody neighborhood is enamored of spies. I am not a spy. I simply visited here today, so I could get a look at the place. Sandy Krofft is the person with spies." She was so wrapped up in expressing ladylike ire that it took a minute to register Spiros's scowl.

"What kind of talk is that? What do you know about the Krofft woman?"

"Very little, I assure you," Margaret said. "I am a friend of Mrs. Hoopes. She has arranged to provide amenities for the neighborhood."

"Mrs. Hoopes. Mmm." Spiros seemed to have forgotten Sandy. "She interested in this murder?"

"I imagine she's interested in both of them," Margaret said.

Spiros leaned back and rubbed his fleshy chin with his forefinger, then smoothed his mustache. He was not in a hurry, but Margaret was. By now De Vere was surely searching for her among the onlookers at the explosion, being wise enough to know that she would never have stayed behind at Saint Lucy's.

"A curious statement," Spiros said. "Do you know of more than one?"

Margaret was impatient. "If you sent your flunky to capture me, surely he knew about the explosion and heard what was being said. Tommy Falco was found strangled in the rubble, and I seem to recall that he was in your diner this afternoon. You spoke to him."

"For someone who is not a spy, you certainly gather a lot of information," Spiros said. "I don't murder people who eat in my diner, unless the food kills them." He seemed to find his joke funny. Then he sat forward and said seriously, "Listen. I don't like these murders; they're bad for business. But Frances was up to something, and somebody didn't like it. That's all I know. Tommy . . ." He dismissed Tommy Falco with a wide gesture. "Let's discuss why you're here."

"I'd be glad to know," Margaret said. "I can't imagine that we have many matters in common."

"Money," Spiros said simply. "You want to make some money?"

"How?" Margaret asked cautiously.

"I figure you got an in with these developers if you're here tonight. You can help me. I bought up property in the neighborhood with some partners. It was coming onto the market, and I found out in advance. I got it pretty cheap, pulled it right out from under this guy who works for the developer. Thinks he's a big deal."

"So you are acquainted with John Mascarpone," Margaret said.

"I know him," Spiros said. "He's around the neighborhood. I don't want to deal direct with him, you know? So I figure you could be like a go-between. You got, what do you call it? Clout. It's right down the street from the new building, and when they start the next phase, it'll be worth plenty to them."

"Next phase. More buildings, you mean."

"Oh, sure. The plans are all done. Big project. This building is nothin'. They're buying up property like crazy. They got people helping. . . ."

Margaret took a risky stab in the dark. "Are you speaking of Castrocani or Sandlot? Or both?"

Spiros didn't answer.

"Could it be," Margaret asked, "that you've been dealing with these people, and now you'd rather they didn't find out you were doing business on your own as well?"

He still didn't answer her question, but he had a faint smile. "A lot of people have been talking about selling out."

"Perhaps you've also been assisting in making the owners more desirous of selling? A bit of harassment and unpleasantness, some actual threats here and there? Possibly even a bomb or two?"

Spiros looked shocked. "I wouldn't do anything like that."

Margaret said, "Someone appears to be doing it. And someone's killing people in the neighborhood who are involved with the building one way or another, or who know something. Now I find that you can't really explain yourself."

Spiros frowned again. "I don't want any of these guys sore at me," he said. "I don't want to end up dead. You work for *Ms.* Krofft and Mascarpone. We're talking about tough as steel."

"I don't actually work for the firm." But of course she did, in a sense. She had a large check to prove it.

Spiros shrugged. "I can look out for myself, but I got other people to answer to, you know? Business partners. They don't like trouble. So you'll help me out? I got to unload this property. It's a financial drain. I'll pay you well."

Margaret thought a minute. Apparently there was considerable work available for a free-lance go-between.

"I don't think I can help much," Margaret said. "Miss Krofft is not likely to attend to anything I say. What if I spoke to Mrs. Hoopes, since she's the principal owner of the company?" Margaret had no idea whether Carolyn Sue cared one way or another about how property was acquired for her company or whether she wanted to acquire more, but agreeing seemed a good way to get herself out of this warehouse and safely back to De Vere.

"Talk to whoever you want. Just help me out. I'll make it worth your while." Spiros attempted to look menacing as he leaned forward over his desk, but he was merely a worried, slightly overweight, middle-aged man trying to protect his doubtful business interests.

Margaret stood up. "I'd like to get back to my friend now."

"Yeah, the cop. You know, I remember him when he was younger, and I was . . . well, younger myself. You going to tell him about this?"

"He's not here in any official capacity," Margaret said. "Just as a good friend." She stood up, ready to face the long, dark street between here and the explosion site.

"Aha." Spiros smiled. "Boyfriend? Whaddaya know. Say, aren't you going to ask how much?"

"I'd prefer to trust you," she said.

"Good. One person you can trust is Spiros."

Spiros must have pressed a signal button on his desk, because Margaret's escort reappeared. "Take Lady Margaret Priam back where you found her. Treat her good."

Margaret smiled. "You're pretty good at getting information, too, Spiros."

"Why do you say that?"

"You've never heard my name, at least not from me and not at the meeting, since you didn't even come into the room."

He waved his hand. "Ah, well. You hear things." He

walked with her to the door. "You give me a call when everything's fixed up. Here's my card."

"Oh, I certainly will," Margaret said. "Acme Import/Export. Exactly what do you import and export, then?"

He smiled. "Olive oil. Kalamata olives. *Comboloi*—worry beads, you know? Lots of Greeks in Astoria and Flushing. All around New York. They all got to eat, and they all worry."

Outside the warehouse, Margaret said to her escort, "I will be able to find my way."

The man shrugged. "Spiros said to take you back. You got to be careful around here at night." The headlights of a fairly substantial truck caught them as it turned into the street. "These delivery guys don't follow no traffic rules. Come on."

He marched her briskly toward the better-lighted street where she had last seen De Vere conferring with his colleagues. If he had returned to the parish hall and found that she had gone, he would not be pleased. He would tell her why, in that calm way of his, and she would feel chastened and remarkably safe in his hands.

Not for the first time in recent days did she wonder if she had been spending rather too much time with him, coming to rely on his apparently balanced view of the way things worked. However, she didn't imagine that he talked out loud to himself in the apartment in Chelsea and regretted that Margaret wasn't around to tell him to be more frivolous and less policemanlike.

"I'll leave you here," the man said. "I got to get back to the warehouse."

"Another truck full of Kalamata olives to unload, I expect," Margaret said, but her attention was on the diminished cluster of official vehicles and the straggling remains of the curious.

"Olives? Oh, yeah. Take care now." He walked off briskly.

De Vere was still standing with a uniformed policeman, but he came to her as soon as she approached.

"It wasn't wise to wander off," he said. He was mildly annoyed at having briefly mislaid her. "Father Steve told me you left the parish hall some time ago."

"I was here. Then I met a friend," Margaret said. "I was just down the street."

Margaret hadn't decided how to deal with Casey's information about Tommy's plan to meet with someone who might have murdered him. Sandy Krofft lurking in a limousine. Her strange visit with Spiros. Gradually seemed best.

The last hard-core rubberneckers were waiting near the demolished building to see if any further sensations were in store. The news-at-eleven television people had departed.

"They found a body," De Vere said. "Not killed by the explosion."

"Strangled. I heard," Margaret said. "You know what New York is like," she added defensively when De Vere looked at her questioningly. "There are no secrets. Not on the broad avenues of Manhattan or the narrow streets of Arcadia."

"Then you also know it wasn't a gas explosion but some kind of bomb. The bomb squad was all over the place. Not a professional job."

"And how are the bomb and the dead man connected?"

"Nobody knows yet. Maybe the bomb was a nuisance gesture that was more effective than planned."

"I'm sure the police will figure it out. We could leave now. Life in the boroughs outside of Manhattan can be tiring."

De Vere faced her, with his hands on her shoulders. "Are you all right? You seem . . ."

"Confused," she said. "And disappointed that I didn't do my job for Carolyn Sue. I dread calling her tomorrow."

He looked at his watch. "It's not very late. Want to go someplace where we can sit knee to knee and you can tell me what's bothering you?"

Margaret laughed. "My knee is your knee, Sam. What about that Irish bar you mentioned?"

"As long as you don't tell the bartender that you're English. If it's the same guy, he was partial to the IRA."

They walked back toward Saint Lucy's, where De Vere had parked his car. Margaret decided to start with the easy part.

"I was surprised to see Sandy Krofft here tonight. Carolyn Sue's woman at Castrocani Development. She told me she wasn't going to be here, but I saw her lurking in a chauffeured car around the explosion site."

"Perhaps she didn't choose to tell Carolyn Sue's agent what she intended to do."

Margaret was grateful to be safely in the passenger seat of the car, even though it was colder inside than out.

Margaret said as De Vere started the car, "I don't imagine Carolyn Sue's company goes in for after-hours demolition of buildings it owns, do you?" Then she added, almost under her breath, "Unless it was a cover-up for murder."

De Vere looked at her sharply. "I said they didn't know that."

"There was a young woman at the meeting tonight, the photographer. . . ."

"I noticed her," he said. "Cute."

"Do you think so? She told me she spoke this afternoon to the man who was killed. A neighborhood layabout named Tommy Falco. It seems he told her that he'd witnessed Frances Rassell's murder some nights ago, and he was to meet someone this evening who was to pay him off to keep silent."

"Mmm." De Vere tested his brakes against the snow-covered streets, which hadn't been plowed and perhaps never would be if the city was hoping for a quick February thaw.

"I told her she should speak to the police."

"Good advice," he said.

"Aren't you interested?"

"Oh, yes," he said, "but it's not my case."

"Somebody's going around strangling people," Margaret said, somewhat indignant. "She knows something about it."

"All right," he said. "If you want the police to call upon this friend who says she heard something from a person now dead who said he saw something, I could call a couple of people. However, if you let nature and the law take their course, the detectives will be around tomorrow morning asking questions. People will have an opportunity to report anything they might know. You told her what to do."

"All right," Margaret said. "For the present. I was just worried that she might be in danger if, say, the murderer saw her with Tommy this afternoon. They were right there together in the street near the construction site."

Happily, De Vere was halted at a red light, so he could turn and stare at her. "They were *where*? How do you know that?"

"I saw them," Margaret said. "I came across earlier today to have a look at the neighborhood. Casey Teale showed me about. I'd met her the other night at the reception for Dianne Stark's committee." Margaret remembered Spiros. "Some quite interesting people in the neighborhood. I even had a chat tonight with your friend Spiros."

"He's been skirting the law for years," De Vere said. "A real character."

"I have an idea," she said. "Would your IRA-sympathizing bartender know who makes homemade bombs hereabouts? I say, De Vere, this street takes us to the bridge and back to Manhattan."

"I think I'll find another place to sit knee to knee," he said. "Someplace where you won't be thinking about bodies discovered in the snow and who can make a pipe bomb out of a few simple household items."

Margaret was rather relieved that there would be no more talk that evening about murders.

"Your place has a working fireplace, doesn't it? Paul's still out of town, and I seem to recall seeing a stack of those odd artificial logs that burn with pretty colors."

"Done," De Vere said. "And I managed to wash the dishes since your visit the other day."

De Vere's apartment was in a four-story, gray stone town house from an earlier, more spacious and gracious era with a sturdy, young pine tree with snowy branches planted in a miniscule square of earth in front of it.

He unlocked the door from the street. In the downstairs

hall, the sound of Mahler seeped out from the ground floor apartment inhabited by a serious, silent, middle-aged man Paul had introduced her to. They started up the nicely carpeted stairs to the next floor, where De Vere and Paul's duplex began. De Vere stopped abruptly midway up the stairs.

"I think," he said, "that we are not alone."

"Surely Paul wouldn't leave the tropics to return to New York at this time of year," Margaret said. "Unless he has managed to find a new job, or unless he's met some lush and wealthy wench with a craving to see Manhattan in winter."

De Vere pointed to the fanlight above his door. Lights were on in the apartment. "I left it dark," he said.

"Do we knock and see who answers, or do we burst in? Perhaps robbers are attempting to make off with Paul's CD player and those very expensive cuff links and studs Carolyn Sue gave him for Christmas. In that event, shouldn't I feel especially safe since you are with me?"

"I dislike violence," De Vere said. "Why don't you hang back a bit." He proceeded upward and paused to listen at the door. Then he signaled Margaret to follow. "If someone is looting the place, he is enjoying some soft-rock background music."

He tried the doorknob. The door opened.

"Who's there? Bless me, it's Sam!" Carolyn Sue Dennis Castrocani Hoopes bounded into the small foyer with arms outstretched. She was well tanned and dressed in winter white, from the tips of her white suede boots to the silver fox collar on her nubby white wool suit. Her hair was even blonder than Margaret remembered.

"Carolyn Sue, what a surprise," Margaret said. "You were in Jamaica at noon today."

"Our little cabana was *right* next to this lovely man whose private jet was jes' settin' at the airport doin' nothin'. Ah felt Ah had to get here and see that things were straightened out. Ah told him Ben and Ah would be happy to repay the favor sometime, when we had our own little jet with us. Sam, don't you look as handsome as can be? Paul stayed in Jamaica with his stepdaddy; I like seeing those two together. Ben says you've been a real grand influence on the boy." Carolyn Sue's Texas accent, which ebbed and flowed like the tides, was in full flood.

"Don't jes' stand there. Y'all come on and rest yourselves. Ah'm only goin' to stay a day or two, Sam, if it won't trouble you. The Villa d'Este is nearly full up, and some movie gal is stayin' there—y'all know the one I mean, ran off with the fellow who was set to marry someone else right on the weddin' day. He's there, too, so the paparazzi are simply besiegin' the place. Good for business—" Carolyn Sue, as part owner of the Villa d'Este Hotel, was fond of seeing high occupancy figures on the reports. "Ah don't like pushin' my way through crowds. I'll lay my head down in Paul's room."

When Carolyn Sue paused to take a breath, De Vere said, "No trouble at all, Carolyn Sue. You own this house."

"You know, you're right," Carolyn Sue said as she led them from the foyer into the living room. "Now, Margaret, Ah was expectin' to see you tomorrow, but now you're here, you can tell me every little thing about tonight."

Margaret looked at De Vere and sighed. "I'm afraid I have rather bad news about tonight, Carolyn Sue."

"Ah can take it, good or bad," Carolyn Sue said. "You can tell us both."

"Us?" Margaret said faintly.

"Why, yes." Carolyn Sue flung out her hand, and the lamplight caused the diamonds on her fingers to blaze like little shooting stars. "Ah called Sandy Krofft to come around here tonight for a chat, seein' as Ah'm only in town for a day or two. She'll want to hear what y'all have to say."

Chapter 13

Margaret's first thought as Sandy glided in was that she had rarely been in a room with so much overpowering blondness.

Her second thought was that Sandy Krofft was looking at De Vere the way one of Priam's Priory's stable cats would examine a particularly tasty-looking, defenseless bird. At least she restrained herself from pouncing.

Almost restrained herself. She went to De Vere with hand outstretched. "I'm Sandy Krofft. We haven't met."

All right, Margaret thought. He's an attractive man, so naturally she's attracted.

"Sam De Vere," he said. He tried to make the handshake brief, but Sandy clung as long as she could. De Vere looked at Margaret out of the corner of his eye and grinned ruefully.

"Surely you're not the policeman Lady Margaret hired on as her driver." At least Sandy refrained from batting her eyelashes and looking coy.

"I forced myself upon her," De Vere said.

"Listen to him," Carolyn Sue said. "Sam is about the nicest man you could meet. If it weren't that I've got my Ben and Margaret's got Sam, I'd make a mighty serious play for him. Y'all come along and sit down. We got to hear this bad news."

"Bad news?" Sandy said. "About the meeting tonight?"

She was a good actress. If Margaret hadn't known what Sandy must know, she might have believed in Sandy's surprise.

"I thought surely you of all people would have heard," Margaret said sweetly. "I understood you to say that you had spies in the neighborhood." She wondered if Sandy would ever admit to being in the neighborhood tonight.

"I don't keep in constant touch," Sandy said smoothly. "I certainly don't have a network of spies over there."

They sat in the chairs in front of the fireplace, but the idea of a cozy fire for two had faded now that Carolyn Sue and Sandy had joined the party.

Carolyn Sue leaned forward. "Margaret, honey, you tell us everything." She was ready to listen closely, no longer the dithery southern belle, but someone whose money was at stake.

Margaret told them almost everything: the complaints about the vandalism and threats to the property owners, the damage that some said would be done by the blasting.

"One fellow mentioned the decline of the quality of life," she said.

"Quality indeed," Sandy muttered.

"And a man named Arthur Cramdell caused quite a stir by announcing that Frances Rassell had been in the pay of Castrocani Development." She watched Sandy as she said this, but the reaction was predictable.

"Absolutely untrue," Sandy said. "I told you I met the woman perhaps once. I was not impressed by her."

"He also said that someone tried to run him down this very night."

"Delusions," Sandy said. She was definitely coolheaded in the face of unwelcome words.

"Perhaps your Mr. Mascarpone had something to do with it?"

"Johnny is barely able to tie his shoes," Sandy said.

"I do believe that every time I've seen John, he has been wearing nice Gucci loafers," Carolyn Sue said.

"Which proves my point," Sandy said.

"Just as I was about to announce your generous gift to the community," Margaret said, "somebody blew up an empty building down the street from Saint Lucy's."

"Good lord!" Carolyn Sue exclaimed. "What next?"

"I understand," Margaret said, "that the building that was destroyed was actually owned by you, Carolyn Sue."

"Well, I never . . . Me?"

"That short block of empty houses across from the construction site," Sandy said. "We bought out the last holdout two months ago. Demolition was scheduled for the spring."

Margaret blinked at Sandy's slip. De Vere was watching her with considerable interest that had nothing to do with her fetching short skirt that showed a well-turned ankle, a shapely calf and knee, and a rather obvious stretch of thigh.

"So you do have a spy or two," Margaret said. "Or whatever you call them."

"I made an informed guess," Sandy said. "I do, after all, run the company, and I know the territory."

"Yes, but there is one more thing," Margaret said. "A man was killed."

There was no reaction from Sandy.

"Is this one going to be blamed on my poor little ol' building, too?" A look of genuine concern appeared on Carolyn Sue's well-managed face, which was confronting her late forties with all the cosmetician's art that money could buy.

"Inevitably, there will be more talk against your project." De Vere spoke up. "Indications are that this man was strangled prior to the explosion, which might have been intended to hide the murder but failed to do so. Word of that will get around fast enough."

"Strangled? That's how that poor woman was killed." Carolyn Sue looked at Sandy, then Margaret. "It's a conspiracy."

"Don't start making it worse than it is," Sandy said. "There's no connection."

Margaret was about to state the connection but stopped.

De Vere said, "Carolyn Sue, the police will look into the matter very carefully. And you, Miss Krofft, will be fielding plenty of questions, whether or not you think the two murders are connected." He glanced at Margaret, and she could read clearly in his expression a warning not to say anything about why Tommy had supposedly been where he was when he was killed.

"I don't normally partake of spirits at this hour," Carolyn Sue said, "but I feel a bit faint." She did seem pale beneath her high-priced tan. "Perhaps Paul keeps chilled champagne on hand? A sip of Drambuie or the like would do in a pinch."

"I spend little time reviewing the refrigerator," De Vere said, "but I'll see what's there." He cast another look at Margaret, as if to say, "Keep what you know to yourself."

As he headed for the kitchen, Carolyn Sue said in a near whisper, "Margaret, honey, what is Sam sayin'? I had no idea what I was comin' back to. How could this be happenin' to poor me?"

Margaret sympathized, but Sandy stood up wearing a look that conveyed pure contempt for her employer's feminine flutterings. "This business is a bother, but it's irrelevant. A couple of accidents that have no bearing on what we're trying to do over there. The neighborhood is at a dead end. Our job is to revive it, bring in fresh blood, make it live again."

Make a profit, Margaret thought, and what becomes of the old blood that's driven out?

"But *two* murders! They couldn't have been accidents. They must be connected."

"Carolyn Sue, we don't know that there's a connection between Frances Rassell and a broken-down alcoholic."

Margaret wondered how well Sandy had known Tommy Falco.

"I feel personally responsible," Carolyn Sue said, "and Margaret here never got a chance to tell all those folks what I was plannin' to do for them."

Sandy looked toward the kitchen. "They'll find out, one way or another. I'll see if I can help Mr. De Vere."

Sandy did not strike Margaret as a helpful type, but she

was glad to see her leave, so she had a chance to speak alone to Carolyn Sue.

"You must understand, Carolyn Sue," Margaret said, "that the community over there isn't at all pleased with the building or eager to be patronized by people like you with more money and power than they have. They don't want a rich Texas mummy to take care of them. Someone is causing trouble that's going to make your business more difficult. And there's more going on at Castrocani than meets the eye. Do you really trust Sandy?"

"I don't get your meaning."

"I mean, is she so dedicated to the project that she would arrange to kill off the competition? Would she risk a lot to keep quiet someone who might interfere with her plans?"

"Are you sayin' that Sandy is responsible?"

"I don't know," Margaret said. "In spite of what she claims, she knows exactly what happened over there tonight. She knew who was killed. She was over there in Queens tonight. I saw her at the back of the parish hall, then in a car close to the explosion, talking on her car phone."

"That doesn't prove anything, but I'm speechless," Carolyn Sue said, and continued to speak. "I did talk to her on her car phone tonight. She said she was on her way home from some dinner party. That's when I asked her to come round here."

"Let's keep mum about what I've just told you," Margaret said, "until we can sort things out."

"If you say so. But somebody's killin' people over there, and it's tainting my reputation. Whatever am I to do?" Carolyn Sue twisted the enormous diamond on her left hand. She didn't have to "do" anything, of course, but it was endearing that she thought she ought to.

"We'll find a time to talk privately," Margaret said. "They'll be back any minute. I hope." It seemed to be taking some time to open a bottle of champagne.

"Don't you worry about Sandy," Carolyn Sue said, happy to be back on the safer ground of discussing pretty, predatory women. "She has this habit of prowlin' around after men she finds to her likin', but I should think Sam can handle her. And you can as well."

"If you say so," Margaret said, and was relieved to see De Vere and Sandy reappear with champagne in a bucket and a handful of tall champagne flutes. Sandy seemed to have turned all fluttery and girlish, which was definitely not the way to Sam De Vere's heart.

"Sit over here by me, Sandy, honey," Carolyn Sue said firmly. "Let's try to figure out what we ought to do." She examined the label on the dark green bottle and nodded with approval. "At least my dear boy knows a bit about the finer things in life. If only he'd settle down . . ." She poured champagne and sipped it, and looked a bit happier. "I suppose Margaret could catch the killer for us. . . ." She stopped at the sight of De Vere's face. "What I meant to say was . . ."

"I wouldn't dream of interfering with the investigations of the police, Carolyn Sue," Margaret said. "Isn't that right, Sam?"

"Absolutely," De Vere said. "I don't think I'll share the champagne, Carolyn Sue. I'll be driving Margaret home shortly, and then I have some police business downtown."

"Now that we've heard Margaret's news, such as it is, I'll be running along myself," Sandy said. "Carolyn Sue, you and I will meet early tomorrow at the office to plan our strategy. There's sure to be negative fallout in the press about this alleged murder, but we can control that. The architect is coming in at ten, so you'll also have a chance to see what disasters he's been creating."

"Can you be there early, Margaret?" Carolyn Sue asked.

Sandy interrupted. "I think this is really a company matter, Carolyn Sue."

"Margaret has a really sharp brain," Carolyn Sue said, "and besides, she's sort of on the payroll, isn't she?"

"Such a pity we couldn't give Sandy Krofft a lift," Margaret said cheerfully as De Vere started the engine. A gentle snow had started to fall again, but it was late enough that traffic was light. The scene would be peaceful and pretty for the next few hours until Manhattan awoke and churned the whiteness into mushy gray slush.

"A somewhat frightening woman," De Vere said. "Good-looking, though."

"If she interests you, I guess it's not my business to interfere."

"You upper-class English girls are so polite and well bred," De Vere said. He was also rather cheerful.

"That sort of attitude tidily disguises moments of rage that might otherwise upset the servants and the horses," Margaret said. "Would you mind awfully if I went to this meeting tomorrow? I won't be out looking for a murderer, but I might find out something that would be useful. There are things going on that I don't understand."

"You know how I feel."

"And now that you've met Sandy Krofft, doesn't she seem capable of overstepping the bounds of what you'd call well-bred behavior?"

"I find it hard to believe that a woman in Miss Krofft's position would engineer murders for the greater glory of Castrocani Development, if that's what you're thinking," De Vere said. "On the other hand, she may have ambitions we know nothing about. I still don't like the idea of sitting by while you walk into a possible nest of murderers bright and early tomorrow morning."

"Oh, Sam, it's in midtown Manhattan. Uniformed men in the lobby. Vast, silent elevators. An office got up like a Renaissance brothel. Instant espresso service. Ankle-deep carpeting. Architects, receptionists, secretaries. And Carolyn Sue. Surely you don't think she's involved, poor thing. She's been a good friend, and *I* can't sit by and let her face this business alone. She may trust Sandy Krofft, but I don't, murder aside."

"All right," De Vere said. "Go to the meeting. I don't

know why I'm debating it, since you'll do what you choose. You do owe it to Carolyn Sue to be there.''

"I do,'' Margaret said, and remembered Carolyn Sue's substantial fee. ''Indeed I do.''

Chapter 14

In the way the weather performs remarkable changes of pace in New York in February, by the next morning the clouds had blown away, the temperature had risen, and the snow had vanished. The sky was clear, and the breeze was warm and carried a duplicitous promise of spring just over the horizon.

Margaret began the day out of sorts: What to wear on this off-season day that had popped up between winter and spring? What to say to Carolyn Sue and the fearsome Sandy? How to find out exactly what was actually stirring beneath the surface of Castrocani Development and the little neighborhood across the river? The building was beginning to seem more an excuse than a reason for unfortunate happenings of recent days.

She put the participants into a mental list.

Sandy seemed to have few limits to her ambition, capable of any type of murderous behavior, any daring scheme.

Spiros had gotten himself into some mess relating to Castrocani Development that he'd decided Margaret could get him out of. He could well be one of Sandy's spies—and seemed a likely candidate for instigator of the organized vandalism. Murder was something else.

John Mascarpone might do Sandy's bidding; or he might have an agenda of his own that included killing off problems.

The rest of them—Casey, the Wellingtons, the big man named Ernie, poor Arthur, greedy Alice, and who knew who else—needed further consideration. None of them seemed to have cared much for Frances. All of them might have known Frances was playing a double game, if what Arthur said was true.

Arthur claimed that Frances had been spreading tales about his mental health. That might have made the life of a sensitive soul quite unpleasant. Mental aberrations were taken rather more seriously by Americans than by Margaret's countrymen. Margaret's great-aunt Fiona, for example, had adored horses to the point of madness and had ended up thinking she was a brood mare. Poor Great-aunt Fiona was allowed to bed down quietly in the stables and restrict her diet to a variety of grain products.

"I must go over there again," Margaret said out loud, "and find out what is really going on."

The news of a second death in that part of Queens had occasioned a dramatic, if somewhat uninformative, sound bite on the late TV news the night before; a "mysterious" death and explosion rated a short, none-too-thoughtful story in the tabloids. *The Times*, of course, had chosen to ignore the whole business. With showers of stray bullets cutting down innocent bystanders around the city and spectacularly dismembered corpses turning up in trash bags, it must not have seemed like much of a story. If someone had summoned the press last night in advance for publicity purposes, the publicity machine wasn't producing much eye-catching copy.

Margaret paused in her preparations. Rebecca Wellington was definitely a publicity-related person, but since she was eager to be on the good side of Castrocani Development, it did not seem that promoting a minor disaster involving the firm would produce a healthy relationship. Unless . . . Margaret thought again. Unless it was a way of proving to Sandy that she could summon the press for good or ill. Margaret would have to see if she knew how to make a bomb for public relations purposes. Or if her obviously devoted husband knew how.

In spite of what De Vere had said, Margaret remained concerned about the safety of Casey Teale. She could so easily have been seen talking with Tommy Falco by the person who had finished him off.

She would go to Arcadia after she had seen Carolyn Sue and Sandy. She set out for the offices of Castrocani Development somewhat earlier than she had been commanded to arrive. She hoped for a chance to chat up Dawn, the receptionist, before meeting with the ladies of the firm.

"Good morning, Dawn," Margaret said. The second time around, the offices of Castrocani Development were easier to take, since one already knew what lay behind the door with the discreet brass plaque that greeted one in the hallway.

Today Dawn was dressed in emerald green with some very noticeable gold jewelry. Her job must pay very well.

"Why . . . Well, good morning, Lady Margaret," Dawn said. "I didn't know you were expected." Margaret saw she was surreptitiously checking a list behind the gleaming marble facade of her desk. "Miss Krofft has a meeting at ten, so she should be here soon."

"And Mrs. Hoopes?"

Dawn looked alarmed. "She's in the Caribbean. Isn't she?"

"A flying trip to New York to look after business," Margaret said. "I'm meeting her here this morning. I should have thought Miss Krofft would have mentioned it."

"She tells me only what she thinks I need to know," Dawn said. Her tone indicated that, of course, she knew a lot more than that.

"I suppose you heard on the telly about the murder in Queens last night," Margaret said. "Or read it in the papers."

"Murder? No murder mentioned in *The Times*." But Dawn was interested.

"Rather like the case of Mrs. Rassell," Margaret said. "I suppose she had occasion to come here fairly often."

"Here? I mean, I don't know her. Coffee will be right out, if you'll take a seat." Dawn quickly suppressed her interest and busied herself answering a phone call.

"She was that older woman who was killed at the new building," Margaret said helpfully when Dawn had completed her phone call. "I understood that she was negotiating on behalf of the neighborhood and met often with Miss Krofft."

"A couple of people from over there have been here," Dawn admitted reluctantly. "I couldn't tell you their names." She had a look that seemed to say, "No more questions."

The arrival of the coffee girl gave Dawn the opportunity to turn her back on Margaret and pick away at a keyboard embedded in the marble behind her desk. No doubt a computer screen was well hidden to keep from spoiling the sense of waiting in Lucretia Borgia's anteroom.

Suddenly the door from the outside swung open wide, and a dapper and self-satisfied John Mascarpone appeared. Margaret looked cautiously at his feet. No Guccis, but another expensive brand of loafers, highly polished black ones with tassels. De Vere also favored loafers, also highly polished, but she was certain he could tie laces if necessary.

Johnny Mascarpone stopped short at the sight of Margaret demurely sipping her espresso and leafing through *Forbes*.

"Well," he said. "Well, well."

"Mr. Mascarpone," Margaret said, "I wonder if you could give me a few minutes before Miss Krofft and Mrs. Hoopes arrive."

"Jeez! Carolyn Sue? Here in New York?" He seemed even more distressed than Dawn at the prospect of Carolyn Sue. "Sure, yeah. I got time. The architect's always late. . . . Carolyn Sue?" Margaret followed him out of the reception area into the long, silent hallway to his office.

"Have a seat," he said. "My usual cappuccino, sweetheart." This was addressed to the coffee girl who hovered at his door. "So." He sat behind his desk and leaned back in his chair.

Although Margaret was not the nubile young wench she imagined he preferred, she thought she could manage him handily.

"I'm going to speak in confidence," she began, "since you obviously represent the . . . the . . . Oh, what *do* I mean? The strong, masculine intelligence that a development company needs. Am I putting this correctly? I don't mean to say that Miss Krofft is not clearly a very, very significant element of the organization."

Yes, Margaret said to herself, I am ashamed, but what's a poor girl to do?

Johnny smiled. "How can I help you? Do I call you Lady Margaret? I don't know about these English titles. The old prince—I told you we were distantly related? Right. He was just *Principe*, whether you were his son or his wife or some poor relation like me, visiting from America. . ."

"You can just call me Margaret," she said as winsomely as possible at an hour before ten in the morning. "My friends call me Margaret."

"That's more like it. And you call me John. So, what can I do for you?"

"I suppose you've heard about the trouble last night," she said.

"Trouble?" He leaned forward over his desk. Margaret thought from his expression that he knew all about it.

"I was prevented from making the generous offer Mrs. Hoopes had decided upon for the neighborhood." She smiled—a little sad, a little regretful. "There was an explosion and a murder. No, no. Silly me. There was a murder, and *then* there was an explosion, according to the police. The dead man was named Tommy Falco. Apparently a harmless neighborhood character who unfortunately saw too much. I say, John, I didn't mean to upset you."

"Swallowed . . . coffee . . . wrong."

He did not seem in need of a Heimlich maneuver, so Margaret kept to her chair.

"How do you know all this? About explosions and murders?" he said as he gulped air and appeared to recover.

"I rushed to the scene. I listened and asked a few questions."

"Yeah, Tommy. He saw everything."

"You knew him?" Margaret was only mildly surprised.

"I knew Tommy, all right," Johnny said slowly. "We go back a long ways. My family lived there for a while when I was a kid, before we moved to Howard Beach. Tommy was older than me, but even back then he was hanging around after Vietnam. He had some kind of job for a while—painter, carpenter, I forget."

"And somebody strangled him. Did you know Frances Rassell, too, from the old days?"

"Margaret . . ." He seemed to relish the first-name basis. She only hoped that he wouldn't decide on a cozy "Meg" or "Peg" or, heaven forbid, "Maggie." Only her cousin Nigel Priam had ever gotten away with calling her that. "I may have seen Frances Rassell around when I was a kid, but I swear I don't remember her. She used to come to the offices to see Sandy, and she mentioned once she'd known my folks. I don't know what her business here was. Sandy doesn't let me in on too much. I don't ask."

She contemplated asking him about Sandlot but thought better of it for the present. Instead she said briskly, "What about Spiros?"

Johnny attempted to look blank.

"I know you know him. What I'm wondering is whether people from that community made a serious attempt to . . . influence you and thereby Castrocani Development? Say by providing opportunities to make a bit of money?"

"I'll be honest with you. I've had a couple of calls. I don't know how they got my name. This guy said he had some property for sale. Wouldn't give his name, so I wasn't going to talk to him. He wanted to know what the property would be worth to me. He said he'd let me have it at a good price, so I could sell it to the company, make a big profit."

"What is it worth?" Margaret asked.

"Couldn't say. I told him I wasn't interested. When we decide to acquire property, Sandy and her lawyers make the approach."

"What if I told you I had a similar offer to make?"

"You?"

"You could buy the property I'm authorized to offer and sell it to Castrocani. I'd do you a favor, and maybe someday you could return the favor. Simple."

He looked at her through narrowed eyes, trying to figure out what she was up to. Finally he said, "Why don't you offer it direct to Sandy and your pal Carolyn Sue?"

So Johnny Mascarpone wasn't readily bribable by the likes of Lady Margaret. He wasn't so dumb.

"I don't do the deals around here," he said. "I do the dirty work. City approvals, the commissioners of this and that, inspections. Now I got these other things coming down the line. We're going to clear out everything and like build a new town over there. You should see the plans. Dynamite town houses. Luxury, you know? With a view of Manhattan. A hotel, a kind of mall. More offices and apartments. We build low rises facing Manhattan and high rises behind. We might go condo right away or keep it rental for a while. We're working on that. Once this first building is finished, they can't stop us. . . ."

"Johnny! You're in early for a change." Sandy moved in like a tornado and cut short the conversation. "I'll just take charge of Lady Margaret. Carolyn Sue is waiting in my office. Come along. Not you, Johnny. Take care of the architect. I'll be with you shortly. We're going to have to see the project manager today as well." She turned and departed.

"Thanks awfully for taking time for me," Margaret said to Johnny, who was staring after Sandy with a look that suggested desire and loathing were at war in the desert of his brain. "I'm simply all at sea about this. I'd hate to have the press get a hint of my involvement. You know how they are. One hint of me mixed up with explosions and murders, and it would be on the telly and in the papers, and word would get back to England to my brother, the earl. I suppose you would know all about dealing with the media. . . .''

"What? Never have anything to do with those guys," he said. "Creeps."

"Perhaps we could meet again sometime for drinks," Margaret said.

"Hey, great." He seemed so eager that Margaret was almost convinced that he had nothing to do with the drama in Queens and indeed was just what he seemed: a slightly dim womanizer who fancied himself the object of all female desire and spent his free time being Sandy Krofft's errand boy.

The coffee girl put her head in the door. "Miss Krofft is insisting . . ."

The girl hustled Margaret along to Sandy's office. A subdued Carolyn Sue was waiting with Sandy, who was drumming her fingers impatiently on the marble top of her desk.

As soon as Margaret sat, Sandy said, "I don't know what nonsense Johnny was telling you, but his knowledge of the project is not to be trusted."

"We were merely chatting," Margaret said, "about this and that."

Sandy dismissed chat with a wave of her well-manicured hand. Her blond hair was pinned up today, and she looked almost delicate and vulnerable.

"Carolyn Sue and I reached some conclusions last evening after you left," she said.

"Ah . . ." Margaret said. Carolyn Sue adjusted the hem of her Karl Lagerfeld skirt and studied the tip of her Charles Jourdan shoe.

"We will prepare a letter to be sent to this community group. I know the priest at Saint Lucy's. Father Steve. We'll have it delivered to him, and he can pass it on to the appropriate persons."

Margaret had a sudden vision of Father Steve rushing coatless through the cold night with the purple stole around his neck to send Tommy Falco to the next world with his sins forgiven.

"Margaret? Are you hearing this?" Carolyn Sue said.

"Yes, yes. Go on."

"What Sandy here is sayin' is we don't think you'll be going over there for another try at makin' my generous donation known to the community."

"We have made other arrangements," Sandy said. "You understand our position."

"I suppose the second murder has made you even more sensitive about your position," Margaret said. "And there are the other matters: the vandalism and the people buying up property so they can resell it to Castrocani Development for a healthy profit."

Sandy looked slightly cross now, as though she had tried to swat an offending housefly and kept missing it. She stood up. "I know nothing about what you're talking about. You always get speculators when a building is going up. The architect is due soon. I'll want you to see him briefly, Carolyn Sue. Nothing too strenuous. Then you can go shopping or something."

"Lovely," Margaret said quickly. "Let's meet for lunch around noon, Carolyn Sue. You haven't seen the new Galeries Lafayette at Trump Tower, have you? Or the new Bendels. It's been ages since you've been in New York. We'll have a good gossip about all our chums. You haven't heard the latest news about Dianne Stark, and I do need your advice about my hair. It's just not right. Perhaps a complete makeover . . ."

Sandy almost sneered at Margaret's babble. "You'll find me in Johnny's office, Carolyn Sue."

"Now, what kind of nonsense are you sayin'?" Carolyn Sue said when Sandy had gone. "Hair and makeovers? I can't just run off and play. There are problems here that need attendin' to."

"Hush," Margaret said. "We do need to talk. Let Sandy Krofft think we have brains made of trifle. I don't trust her an inch, and I don't like what's going on."

"I see! No trouble for me to act like a frivolous fool. I watch these ladies down home doin' it all the time." Carolyn Sue grinned. "I've even been known to behave in that manner toward dear old Ben to get my way. What do you suppose is goin' on over there?''

"I'm not sure," Margaret said. "Also interesting is what's going on here. See you at lunch."

"I'll just go see what Sandy and this architect are up to. I like what he's doing so far. Ben says I have real good taste when it comes to spendin' money on buildings."

Chapter 15

"*I kinda* like Trump Tower, in spite of Donald," Carolyn Sue said. "I don't know anybody who buys a thing here, except maybe at Buccellati, but it does have its own unique style."

Carolyn Sue gazed up at the two-story waterfall that spilled down one side of the Trump Tower lobby, reflecting off the bronze-colored mirrors. The narrow escalators carried lookers, if not buyers, who had wandered in off Fifth Avenue up to the floors of pricey shops and down again to the pinkish orange marble atrium.

Carolyn Sue and Margaret descended one level to the Bistro, the small and not inexpensive restaurant tucked away at the foot of the waterfall, open to the floor where less affluent lunchers sat with trays from the cafeteria-style counter on the opposite side. Carolyn Sue claimed that she couldn't bear to greet the Pats and Judys and Jerrys at Mortimer's or Le Cirque or one of the other ultra-fashionable spots where meals tended to be tiny, but the checks were not. "An' if Harry Dowd knew I was in town, I'd never hear the end of it if we didn't lunch."

"I do understand," Margaret said, as they seated themselves on the red banquettes deep inside the restaurant and far from the comings and goings of the public.

"I don't feel like talkin'," Carolyn Sue said. "Even if they don't know all about my little troubles."

"If Poppy Dill has her grapevine in working order, they probably know everything," Margaret said dryly. "Don't forget, these people are addicted to gossip."

Carolyn Sue raised her eyes to heaven. "Lord, don't I know that." She smiled her big good ol' gal smile at Margaret. "I'm feelin' cheerier already, knowin' that Chanel and Tiffany's and Cartier and Bergdorf's are all within spittin' distance out there on Fifth Avenue."

"That's better," Margaret said. She waited until the waiter who brought their salads was gone. "Did Sandy say anything of interest after I left?"

Carolyn Sue's good humor evaporated. "You're right about something bein' not quite right. I started asking questions about the way money was being spent. Sandy's car and driver, her apartment, which the company seems to be paying for, some mighty high expenses that aren't clear. Now she wants to hire on a public relations firm. . . ."

Margaret listened closely to this. "Did she mention a name?"

"No, but I told her you were public relations enough for the moment."

"I imagine she welcomed that," Margaret said ruefully. "But I haven't really done anything, and I don't think there's much I can do. I'm going to return your check. . . ." It had arrived that morning from Dallas by overnight courier.

"You're not," Carolyn Sue said. "You're going to find out who's murdering people on my behalf over there in Queens. I don't like to go against Sam De Vere, but that's what I want you to do. Please, Margaret."

Margaret sat back and thought. "The police will find the murderer eventually," she said slowly.

"Not good enough. You know there are plenty of cases that are never solved. I don't mean you have to go out and lasso the critter. I jes' want to know who and why. I don't want to put you in danger, but there's got to be some answer that will let me rest easy."

"There seem to be three possibilities," Margaret said. "One, the source of this particular evil is corporate—your company or possibly another. Two, the source lies in the group opposed to your building."

"You are clever," Carolyn Sue said. "What's number three?"

"It has nothing to do with the building at all. A personal attack on Frances, with poor Tommy Falco caught up by accident. Let's start with corporate killers. Anything else from Sandy?"

"Just that she was mighty cross that I questioned her about expenses," Carolyn Sue said. "You understand this has nothing to do with financing the building. Some of that is my money, some is from other investors. We're payin' hefty interest on it, but work is on schedule so far. She was right testy that I was asking any questions at all about the firm, like it was none of my business. The money Sandy's throwin' around is company funds for this building. I don't believe Sandy was born to the finer things, so she sets a great store by them now."

"How did you happen to hire her?"

Carolyn Sue looked uncomfortable. "Johnny Mascarpone brought up her name, I think. She has a very good background in the field; I checked on that."

Margaret was vaguely exasperated. "And how did you and Johnny reach such intimacy that he was recommending chief executives to you?"

"He sorta turned up a couple of years ago. And bein' a relative of Aldo's and all . . ."

"Judging from what I know of the Italian aristocracy, I find that relationship difficult to swallow," Margaret said, "even if his immediate family has lived in America for a couple of generations."

"I wrote to Aldo about him," Carolyn Sue said. She sounded defensive. She was not accustomed to either implied or overt criticism. "Not that I'd let on to Ben, who's a tiny bit jealous of that old marriage of mine."

"And your Prince Aldo told you exactly what?"

"He wrote in Italian, silly man. He knows I never was good at reading it. I was too busy raising Paul in that drafty old villa—I don't know if you've ever spent a winter in Italy in a place built in fifteen hundred and something, but I do believe they hadn't even invented fire back then. Anyhow, I finally made out that Aldo was saying John was some sort of relative, all right."

"He still looks to me," Margaret said, "like a well-dressed gangster." She thought for a moment. "I say, Carolyn Sue, since it's your company, I suppose you can go in there anytime you wish, day or night."

"Why, sure. I have a key. Now let me see, did I take it to Jamaica?" She picked up her Fendi handbag and rummaged through it. She pulled out a heavy gold keychain and shook the half-dozen keys attached. "Not here. I didn't think so. I didn't expect to be in New York, so it's back home in Dallas. Anyhow, I don't remember ever having the need for a key to get in. What do you have in mind?"

"Nothing, I suppose, if you don't have the key."

"Oh, that's no problem. I could ask Sandy for another."

"No! I don't want her thinking you're going to, say, search the files."

"Aha! Well, no problem as I said. I do have servants home in Dallas who get paid a mighty good salary to know where everything is. And there's the overnight mail. You leave it to me." She cocked her head at Margaret. "Am I going to search the files?"

"No," Margaret said. "I am. Do you know if they lock the files? That would be a problem."

Carolyn Sue thought. "I don't think so. Johnny keeps all that construction stuff in his office. No files in Sandy's office. Her secretary sits next door. Nice boy, don't know how he puts up with her. I don't recall files there either. There's only that file room at the end of the hall."

"That's a start on possibility number one. The next step is number two—the neighborhood. For that, I'll have to cozy up to my new best friend."

Carolyn Sue was entering the spirit of the chase. "Who's that goin' to be?"

"A woman named Rebecca Wellington. She's invited me to brunch on Sunday at her house in Queens."

"Why, I never imagined they'd know about a thing like brunch over there."

"It's quite an advanced little community," Margaret said. "Then I ought to look up some other friends in the neighborhood. A nice girl named Casey Teale, for one. Possible help with number three." She didn't want to explain why she was also a bit worried about how Casey was faring and whether she'd told the police her tale of Tommy's rendezvous with his murderer.

The waiter brought desserts. Margaret felt that she was entitled to a sweet, since she had just committed herself to working off the money Carolyn Sue had paid her by finding the truth of two murders.

"There's the matter of the bomb," Margaret said. "How does one make a bomb, and what sort of person knows what to do? Carolyn Sue? Why are you looking as though you've been caught out carrying a knockoff Vuitton handbag?"

"I suppose Johnny would know about explosives," she said in a small voice. "His father was in demolition and construction, he told me. He worked with him for years."

"And where do you suppose he was last night?"

"I could find that out." Carolyn Sue had perked up again. "I'm going back to the office this afternoon, after I do a little shopping. I wouldn't let on why I was askin'."

"I think that would be wise," Margaret said. "Of course, if he doesn't want you to know, he won't tell you the truth. We already know that Sandy was over there."

"No tellin' what Sandy knows. She could be an explosives expert and never let on to me. I'm feeling much better," Carolyn Sue said, "now that I'm being useful." She no longer looked teary, which would have produced a mascara disaster of enormous proportions. "What's this you were sayin' about that darlin' Dianne Stark?"

Carolyn Sue's attention span was not excessive, even when the subject was murder.

When all tales were told about mutual friends and acquaintances and the last bit of chocolate mousse had been disposed of, Margaret and Carolyn Sue rode up the escalators past the waterfall to look in on the Galeries Lafayette. Carolyn Sue said she preferred the one in Paris, simply because it was in Paris. They went out to Fifth Avenue. Carolyn Sue barely paused to admire a huge, pink sapphire ring in the window of Tiffany's. Across the avenue, she wrinkled her nose at the ornate and priceless tiara of some failed empress in a window at Harry Winston.

"Such bad taste," she murmured, "such *badly* cut stones."

They moved on to Henri Bendel, all cream and curves and polite salespeople, and strolled through, but no three- or four-figure designer frock caught Carolyn Sue's eye. The lifelike mannequins posed on balconies and looking out through the tall Lalique glass windows were "downright clever," according to Carolyn Sue, but her heart wasn't in it.

"You could buy something, wear it once, and return it," Margaret said.

"I almost never do returns," Carolyn Sue said grandly, "unless it looks terrible when I get it home and see it in my lighting. If Ben hates it, I'll return it, but I'd never wear a dress and then turn it in like a refund on a pop bottle."

On the avenue again, Ferragamo did not lure her through its doors; the prospect of Bulgari didn't delight her; she turned away from Bergdorf Goodman.

They walked one block over to Madison Avenue, but Carolyn Sue turned down the prospect of venturing uptown to look at the Valentino, Ungaro, Ralph Lauren, and Nicole Miller boutiques.

"Wait for a minute," Carolyn Sue said, and went to a telephone kiosk that had just been vacated by a helmeted bike messenger. Margaret watched her punch in a lengthy series of numbers, speak briefly, and hang up.

"That's done," she said. "Delia knows exactly where my keys are. They'll get to me at Paul's place tomorrow morning." She looked pleased with herself. "I didn't want to be overheard at the office asking for them to be sent."

"You're becoming quite a devious thinker," Margaret said. "Suppose you locate all the files when you go back to the office, and tell me tomorrow."

"I was thinkin' that I have a perfect right to look in any files I choose," Carolyn Sue said. She paused. "Then I thought that might not be such a good idea in front of Sandy and John, especially when I don't know what I'm lookin' for. Do you?"

"Not exactly," Margaret said. "Something. I hope I recognize it when I see it."

With Carolyn Sue heading back to Castrocani Development, Margaret proceeded to her apartment.

At three o'clock in the afternoon, New York was still about its various businesses in offices and mailrooms, behind sales counters and in front of them, at manicurists and hairdressers, finding a seat on a subway car in advance of rush hour, hailing cabs or driving the cabs being hailed.

It was too early to link up with the factions on the other side of the river. She would call Casey Teale in the evening. Rebecca would likely still be at her office, wherever that might be.

Margaret had nothing to do but think. De Vere was somewhere on his police business. Carolyn Sue would soon be leaving the offices of Castrocani Development to return to Paul's apartment in the pale gray-beige stone building on the tree-lined street in Chelsea. She planned to dine out with friends too rich and social even for Margaret. Paul continued to frolic in the blue-green Caribbean. Dianne would be at home with her committee lists waiting for her Charlie.

Margaret had many friends around the city whom she hadn't seen of late, who would be pleased to invite her to join them for drinks or dinner. She couldn't bring herself to call. Afternoon talk shows on the telly, constant news of global disaster on CNN, ancient movies flickering black and white across the screen. None of it appealed to her. Margaret was restless, knowing there were things that had to be looked into. . . .

"Of course!" she said out loud in the direction of the ficus tree bought a few months ago in the hope that it would fill the window with green leaves and a hint of wide country spaces. At the moment, it was suffering from severe leaf drop and looked as much an emblem of winter as the bare, black trees in Central Park or those on the short, pretty street she'd seen in Arcadia.

Dianne Stark was at home.

"Rebecca Wellington? I have the firm's number right here. Feeling the need for some self-promotion?"

"Never," Margaret said. "Someone was inquiring about a good person to handle a sticky public relations problem. You said she was competent." Margaret didn't feel good about her white lie, but she didn't really feel bad either. "I'll tell you about it when I can."

"How about Saturday, twoish? I need help addressing some envelopes on behalf of the committee," Dianne said. "You have that lovely italic hand when you want to. You can tell me then."

"Done," Margaret said. "I say, is Charlie in town? I have a question for him about a business acquaintance."

"Leaving for Washington tomorrow, so you can catch him downtown now. We're dining out tonight."

"With Carolyn Sue?" Margaret hoped not. Carolyn Sue wasn't good at keeping her troubles to herself.

"No, but I heard she'd come to town."

"How gossip does fly from avenue to avenue," Margaret said. "How's the infant-to-be?"

"Ah," Dianne said. "The couturier's challenge, I call her. I want to look smashing at my benefit party, and I will, no matter how large I am. Isn't life wonderful?"

"Mmm." Margaret was noncommittal on that.

She sat back in her comfortable chintz-covered armchair and replaced the receiver.

The two murders in Queens were as much a part of the

huge, incomprehensible mass of the city where she had chosen to live for these last few years as the glittering, sometimes trivial events taking place along the "right" stretch of Park Avenue or in the big apartments on Fifth overlooking Central Park. There was no difference, she thought, between the energy that kept the bright lights of fashionable Manhattan glowing and the pale lamps lit on the dark streets of low warehouses and shabby factories across the river.

She was determined to put a face on the puzzle who made life not so wonderful for people in an unimportant neighborhood, and who could easily, in some other manifestation, take away the joy of Dianne Stark.

Margaret switched on the light against the deepening twilight and reached again for her telephone.

Chapter 16

It was surprisingly easy to get through to Charles Stark. His ultraefficient secretary seemed to know immediately who she was.

"You just caught me," Charlie said. "I'll be gone until next week."

"I need to find out more about Sandy Krofft's background," Margaret said.

There was a pause. Charles Stark did not arrive at his present preeminent position in the financial community by being careless. Margaret was certain that this meant she would not soon see his picture plastered across the newspapers as the latest Wall Street whiz caught in some doubtful if not actually criminal scheme.

"Professional?" he said finally. "I would know nothing of her personal background."

"Professional was what I had in mind."

"I know her only by reputation. Rubs some men the wrong way, others are . . . Ah, never mind. Call these people." He rattled off three names. "My secretary will give you their numbers. It's late in the day, but these guys are so busy building up and tearing down the city, they're likely to keep long hours."

136

"Thanks, Charlie. We must find time for you and me and Dianne to get together."

"Are you still seeing that police fellow?"

"Regularly," Margaret said.

"Good man. Like his style."

Margaret telephoned Casey but heard only the answering machine and left a message.

Rebecca Wellington, in contrast to Charles Stark, was only reached via a long series of suspicious queries from receptionists, secretaries, and assistants. Perhaps that made the caller all the more grateful when she finally came on the line.

"Margaret! What a *nice* surprise." Today, Rebecca's thrill at hearing Lady Margaret's voice had a false ring to it.

"I was doing up my social calendar for the next couple of weeks," Margaret said, never having had such a thing in her life. "You mentioned brunch. Sunday?"

"Ah yes, I did, didn't I?" Rebecca was briefly at a loss. As Margaret had suspected, the blithely issued invitation was not based on a gathering long planned or the expectation that Margaret would accept. "Yes, of course. Sunday. I never dreamed you'd be free. They . . . they're lovely people, but not really what you're accustomed to."

Margaret imagined that Rebecca was thinking hard about whom she could invite on short notice.

"It would be super to meet some of the neighborhood people—the nicer ones, naturally. I'm quite taken with Arcadia."

"Even with people being murdered as they go about their business?"

Margaret tried out a merry laugh. "I'm sure that will be cleared up in no time, and then Carolyn Sue's lovely building will make all the difference in the world. I lunched with her today. Did you say you knew her?"

"Only in passing," Rebecca said. "Is one o'clock on Sunday all right with you?"

"Perfect," Margaret said, and wrote down the address. "Did you get your photos from Casey?"

"What? Oh, from the reception. Yes. She finally slipped

them through our mail slot early this morning. There are some quite charming ones of you. I'll show them to you on Sunday.''

Two of the three men Charlie Stark had suggested she call were in their offices. Both were wary about commenting on Sandy Krofft. ''Capable woman'' was the cautious comment of both.

''I'm on the brink of becoming involved with Castrocani Development,'' Margaret said to both, ''and I want to be sure.''

''I've known Ben Hoopes for decades,'' one of the men told her. ''And his wife. She's done well in real estate, mostly in the Sunbelt and California. Started to diversify when oil got chancy. They know their business.''

''But Miss Krofft . . .'' Margaret decided to be persistent.

Her informant hesitated. ''She's been with some of the big guys,'' he said finally. ''Worked her way up in a tough business for women. The trades and construction professions are pretty much filled with men. On the other hand, Krofft has sometimes been able to use that to her advantage.'' He left it at that.

So, nothing about Sandy Krofft that anybody was willing to talk about.

''One question,'' Margaret said quickly, before he could hang up. ''John Mascarpone.''

''Don't recognize the name,'' the man said, almost too readily. ''I hate to cut you off, Lady Margaret. . . .''

''Thank you so much for your time,'' Margaret said.

It was after five now as Margaret called Acme Import/ Export. Spiros, like the deconstructors of New York, seemed a likely candidate for keeping long hours. A chirpy female voice answered: no Spiros. The number was a well-concealed answering service, but Margaret knew. She left a precise message: ''Call Lady Margaret tomorrow morning between nine and ten.''

Thus far, it was a fairly unproductive afternoon, but tomorrow, with luck, Carolyn Sue would have the key to the office, and tomorrow night, Margaret could make a stab at investigating the company files.

She paced the room. There had to be something else she could do. Then she had it. Telephone information in Queens had a telephone number for F. Rassell in Arcadia. She dialed and found herself talking to Frances Rassell's daughter, Alice.

It took a moment for Alice to get a fix on who Margaret was, and when she did, she sounded moderately hostile.

"I didn't hear nothing about that tribute to Ma," she said.

"No tribute per se," Margaret said, then added hastily, "not to say that Mrs. Hoopes does not feel very strongly indeed about the tragedy."

"What do you want from me?"

"I wanted to ask, Mrs. . . . . ah . . . I'm sorry. I don't know your married name."

"Pirelli," Alice said. "Took Ma years to get used to the idea that I married an Italian and somebody from outside the neighborhood as well."

"Mrs. Pirelli, I didn't have a chance to speak to you personally last evening, with the explosion happening as it did, but I do want to offer my condolences. . . ."

"Words," Alice said sharply. "You can tell your bosses that we're going to sue."

"I'm not the person with whom you should discuss such matters," Margaret said, "but I do want to talk with you."

"Me? What about?" Alice sounded both suspicious and interested.

"About your mother," Margaret said. "The neighborhood. And did you happen to find some photos among your mother's effects? They would be black and white, taken by her neighbor, Casey Teale."

Alice hesitated. "I'm real busy. The funeral is on Saturday, and we got calling hours tonight at the funeral home. Look at the time. I should be there now. Seven to nine tonight. We're expecting a lot of people, but if you come, I could get away for a couple of minutes."

"All right," Margaret said. "And the photos?"

"There's something like that around here. They didn't look like much to me. Ugly. I like colored pictures."

"If you could bring them, I'll see that they're returned to Casey."

Alice rattled off the address. Someplace in Queens, but Margaret had no idea where.

"I'll try to be there by eight," she said. Somehow she would find the place, even if it required her to resurrect her seldom-used car from its parking spot in the basement beneath her building. There was no need to involve De Vere in this venture into the depths of Queens.

She was viewing suitably somber clothes to wear at Frances Rassell's visiting hours and simultaneously poring over a tattered map of the five boroughs of New York to locate her destination when the telephone rang.

"Is this Lady Margaret Priam?" an unfamiliar male voice asked. She was disappointed in her hope that De Vere had found time to ring her.

"You don't know me," the man said. "I saw you at the meeting last night. I didn't hear you speak, but Peter Wellington told me about you. My name is Arthur Cramdell, and I have to talk to you."

"Yes, Mr. Cramdell." She had forgotten him as a source of information. "I believe that might be valuable. I'm calling on Mrs. Rassell's family this evening at the funeral home. I don't suppose you'd care to join me?"

Arthur responded with the sound of strangled horror.

"Ah. I didn't think so," Margaret said. "I don't expect to be long. Perhaps we could meet after, since I'll be in Queens. Your place?"

"No!" Arthur said quickly. "That is, I'm on the top floor above the Wellingtons. I'd rather they didn't . . ."

"I understand," Margaret said. She hadn't known that he lived in such close proximity to the Wellingtons, and she herself didn't care to be seen by them visiting him. "I'm afraid the only landmark I know is the diner. As I will have my car, perhaps I could pick you up there. Would nine-thirty be too late?'' That would give her time to get lost on the mysterious dark streets around Arcadia.

"Yes. I mean, no,'' Arthur said. "The diner. I'll be out in front at nine-thirty.''

Margaret tried to imagine what a very nervous Arthur Cramdell needed to see her about so urgently.

She decided that her charcoal gray suit would be appropriate after all. She brought the map to the light to review her route. The bridge was easy, and she thought she remembered the way taken by both the taxi and De Vere to reach Arcadia. She managed to locate the street of the funeral home and memorized its relationship to Carolyn Sue's building. She was sure she could manage it without becoming hopelessly lost. Probably.

Before she left, she tried Casey Teale's number again. Again she heard only the answering machine. Margaret did not leave a second message.

Morrissey's Memorial Home was a four-story brick building on a street crowded with mid- and down-scale stores: delis, florists, a liquor store, two video stores, a bank, and two or three fast-food places. She noticed an Indian grocery and a Cuban-Chinese restaurant. The urban pot was melting a rather wide range of ingredients. Parking meters lined both sides of the street, but most spaces were empty. Many of the stores were closed for the night and barricaded with metal shutters. The only action in the vicinity was at a tavern a block away.

She parked in the lot behind the building reserved for mourners. Although the funeral home had many regularly placed windows from bottom to top, they were all curtained inside so that no lights showed through.

The heavy door at the entrance opened smoothly, and Margaret found herself in a three-story hall with a marblelike floor. Appropriately mournful rubber plants and potted palms stood against neutral beige walls. Wide stairs on one side carpeted in maroon led to the upper floors, and a signboard with white letters stuck into grooves indicated that the Rassell rooms were on the second floor. There seemed to be no one about on the ground floor as Margaret tiptoed toward the stairs, but she detected the scent of beeswax candles and heard the faint sound of lugubrious organ music.

Upstairs, she paused at the door to the room where another sign indicated that the Rassell family sat within. She peered into the dim room and smelled carnations and other heavy, flowery scents. A number of people were sitting quietly in rows of chairs facing the end of the room, where a dark wooden casket rested on a raised dais. Tall candles burned at either end.

She had not anticipated an open casket. Very different from the English style of upper-class obsequies, where everyone kept upper lips stiff and said the deceased had had good innings, then sent him or her to the final rest with a hymn or two and the vicar—better still, the bishop—saying a few words and reading a bit of Scripture.

"Lady Margaret?" Alice Rassell Pirelli, in severe black but with rather a lot of makeup, touched Margaret's sleeve. "You'll want to have a look at her, so lifelike and peaceful. Poor old Ma. Then we'll talk."

"Well, I didn't know her. . . . That is . . ."

Alice was walking toward the casket. Margaret followed, aware that all eyes were watching her. The organ music that permeated the room seemed to swell as she neared the dais, in case someone had failed to notice her.

Margaret looked down on the remains of Frances Rassell, dressed in a pink dress fussy with lace, with her short, gray hair carefully curled, cheeks a bit too rosy for nature, and her pale hands joined on her breast and holding a rosary. Her mouth was set in a smile, but even in death it seemed smug and just a bit malevolent.

"Lovely. Very peaceful," Margaret said. The room was cold, but Margaret felt flushed and uncomfortable.

She was glad to return to the side of the room, where she was introduced to Alice's husband and her teenage daughter, the latter looking sullen and resentful that she had to waste her evening here. Margaret met Alice's two brothers, large, middle-aged men who looked ill at ease in their dark suits.

"So sorry," Margaret murmured.

One brother nodded; the other stared coldly and said, "How sorry is that company of yours?"

"Frank," Alice hissed, and the brother turned away. "We can talk in the next room. It's not being used," she said to Margaret. "Don't mind my brother. He's taking it hard. He was Ma's baby."

They sat in a room identical to the one they had left, except for an absence of casket, flowers, candles, and organ music.

"What do you want from me?" She was a bit belligerent, now that she was away from her family and her late mother.

"I'm not sure," Margaret said. "Have the police questioned you about your mother's death?"

"Yeah, they did. They asked me who didn't like her, what she was up to about the building. Stuff like that. I don't know anything much about Ma's life, except she was doing that stuff with the neighborhood committee."

"So you had nothing specific to tell them."

"I don't need to tell the cops about my family's business," she said defiantly.

"Nothing about the business Arthur Cramdell spoke about? Being paid on the side by Castrocani Development while she was ostensibly working against the building?"

Margaret thought Alice tensed and reddened behind her elaborate makeup.

"Lies! Of course Ma was careful with her money and put away as much as she could for me and the others. That's no crime. You and I know who killed my mother. Somebody working for that building of yours."

"And she had no other enemies?"

Alice hesitated. "Everybody in the neighborhood knew Ma for years and years."

"Not the newcomers."

"Them. She couldn't stand any of them. She thought they were dragging the neighborhood down with their sex and drugs and art and their interior decorating. Rock music, symphony music, fancy cheese. Poetry! You know what I mean?''

Margaret was amused. "I believe I do. Did she try to drive them away by spreading rumors?''

"You mean that Arthur. She knew for a fact that he's nuts and dangerous. Somebody told her. She knew a lot of things about a lot of people that she never talked about.''

Alice's unfriendly brother stuck his head in the door. "You better get in here, Alice. We can't talk to all these people alone.'' He glared at Margaret as he left.

"I got those photos,'' Alice said. She brought out a brown envelope from her huge bag. "If they're worth money . . .'' she began hopefully.

"I'm afraid not,'' Margaret said. "Casey has the negatives. I'm merely saving her the time of making new prints. I'll be leaving now, so you can get back to your people.'' At the door, she said, "I don't suppose you have information on Sandlot you'd like to share with me.''

Alice looked disgusted. "I should have known. You talk all fancy and English, but you're like all the rest. I got nothing to say.''

Margaret was mildly taken aback but said, "I was merely asking about your mother's interests.''

"She was interested in all kinds of things. No harm in that, is there?''

"Only if you manage to stay alive,'' Margaret said.

Chapter 17

After Margaret left the commercial avenue on which the funeral parlor was located, she drove along quiet residential streets with the window open to the cold night air. Alice hadn't taken long, although the brief meeting had stirred up suspicions. The brown envelope of photos was on the seat beside her, and curiosity about Sandlot was mounting.

Every now and then she caught a glimpse of the tall, lit Citicorp building and knew she was heading in roughly the right direction. If she had remembered her map correctly, she ought to make a left turn soon to place herself somewhere near Arcadia.

At the next stoplight, she thought there was no time like the present and turned left. The short street lined with trees and substantial five- and six-story apartment buildings brought her to another bright commercial street with lively bars and nightclubs, all definitely Hispanic in nature. Then she saw the tracks of the elevated train spanning the road ahead. If she followed its route, she would reach Arcadia.

When she saw the lights of Spiros's diner two blocks away, she realized that she felt as though she had traversed a foreign land and had finally found herself home again.

Down the block she could see the crumbled remains of the demolished house where Tommy Falco had died and across the street, the fencing that marked the spot where Carolyn Sue's new building would rise. A blue-and-white patrol car was parked in front of the diner with a young policeman in the passenger's seat. As Margaret parked across the street, another policeman came out of the diner with a cardboard container of coffee. Two young women with seriously large hair in colors not dreamed of by nature, or indeed any colorist at Bergdorf Goodman, strolled toward the diner laughing uproariously between themselves. They wore thigh-high boots over silver spandex tights and short coats with broad shoulders and big fur collars. Working girls stopping by the diner for a caffeine pick-me-up.

Margaret thought they waved to the police car as it pulled away.

It was only ten minutes past nine, too early for Arthur. She slipped a soothing Mozart piano concerto tape into the player and took a quick look at the photos by the light from a street lamp. They didn't tell her much at first. The four pictures on top were shots of Frances and a crowd of people holding protest signs in front of the fence in the process of being erected at the construction site. Two of Frances looking serious in an equally serious frock posed stiffly on the steps of a neat house. The next three, however, held some interest. One was a picture taken at dusk of a woman in slacks and a windbreaker walking down one of those streets lined with warehouses. Then Spiros and, of all people, Peter Wellington head-to-head in conversation in front of the diner. Finally, a woman in dark glasses breaking away from what looked like an embrace at the door of a car held open by a uniformed driver. Margaret looked again. The image was not distinct, but it looked like Sandy—and the man she was leaving looked like Peter Wellington. They gave her something to ponder as she kept watch for Arthur. She wondered if she should venture into the diner to find him. She was about to open the car door when she saw another woman coming down the street in her direction, a scarf over her head and hunched over with the collar of her coat turned up.

Rebecca Wellington was walking fast and purposefully

through the darkness. She passed the diner and turned down the street beyond it. She might have been out for a brisk walk, but somehow Margaret doubted it. Her walk and demeanor did not convey the image of the young woman executive bent on healthy exercise.

As soon as Rebecca had turned the corner, Margaret was out of the car, locking it behind her. She crossed the street and stayed close to the side of the diner. She could see Rebecca in the distance, heading down a street that Margaret thought must be parallel to the one on which Spiros's warehouse was located. Margaret followed her cautiously.

Like many of the side streets, this one had few streetlights. Cars were closely parked along both sides, but there were apparently no residential buildings, only the blank walls and closed doors of warehouses.

When Rebecca stopped abruptly, Margaret ducked down behind an old Buick with a dangling bumper and masking tape holding the passenger window in place.

She looked over the hood. Rebecca was leaning down to speak to someone sitting in a gleaming, low, and very expensive-looking white sports car. Rebecca was so intent on her conversation that she seemed to be paying little heed to the street around her. Margaret crept carefully along the side of the old car to get a closer look.

She froze at a sound nearby but determined that it was only a mangy-looking dog that skittered away into the night.

Rebecca opened the door of the white car and slipped into the passenger seat. Margaret could just see by the light of a distant streetlight the outline of her head and another, but man or woman she couldn't tell.

Margaret was concentrating on the couple in the car and heard too late the soft footfall behind her. The blow to the back of her head stunned her. She stumbled forward and fell on her face. She heard someone running away. A powerful car engine roared, and through half-opened eyes, she saw the wheels of a car pass by. A wave of pain rolled across the back of Margaret's head, and she closed her eyes. The ground under her cheek was so soothing and cool.

"She not a sister. I never seen her. She doesn't belong here." A woman's voice, a slight accent, perhaps Caribbean. Margaret could not for a moment remember where she was or whether she'd been asleep or unconscious, but now she was awake. The pain remained, but it was diminishing. The new pain, where the sharp, pointed toe of a boot kicked her in the ribs, was startling.

"She dead?" Another woman's voice.

"Not dead," the first woman said. "Mugged. She got anything left?"

Margaret listened in a detached way to them discussing her, not yet quite up to rising. Her bag, in any case, was locked in the car; the keys were in her pocket.

"Quick, Traci, see what's in her pockets."

Margaret felt hands placed on her and decided she ought to test whether her body was capable of doing anything.

"Really! Do stop," she said as forcefully as possible.

"Oh, oh," one said. "We wasn't doing anything, lady."

"You okay?" The woman sounded solicitous now.

Margaret made a great effort and sat up. The two ladies of the night she'd seen entering the diner watched her warily.

"I was attacked." Margaret managed to stand with the aid of the old car. She was slightly groggy but otherwise apparently whole. Thoughts of a concussion arose briefly, but she put them out of her mind. "I seem to be all right," she said, still feeling not entirely all right. "Did you see anyone running away?" She had no idea how long she had been lying on the curb beside the Buick. She looked at her watch. Twenty to ten. Not long, then. She looked down the street. The white car was gone.

The two women shook their heads.

"Guy walking a dog," one said.

"Another guy jogging. You gotta be like, crazy to be running around at night in this city."

"A white car? Sports car, expensive?"

The two women looked at each other, transparently pretending they knew of no such car.

"Do you know who the driver was?"

"No!" they both said quickly. A familiar car then, at least to late-night denizens of the neighborhood.

"Thank you so much for rousing me," Margaret said. She tried a step and found she was able to walk upright and reasonably steadily. She had to get back to meet Arthur Cramdell, but now another figure appeared on the horizon: a man in a heavy overcoat, head down, walking rapidly in their direction.

"Busy street," Margaret murmured.

"You think so?" one of the women said. "It's always slow for us. We're taking a shortcut over to the next avenue. Lots of traffic there." She looked around and saw the approaching man. "Spiros. We don't need none of his talk. Let's go, Veronique." The two women moved off into the night, intent on their business.

"Mmmm, well, well. Lady Margaret." Spiros fingered his mustache and looked her up and down. "Sight-seeing in the neighborhood again?"

"Not really," Margaret said. "Are those young ladies acquaintances of yours?"

Spiros shrugged. "You see 'em around most nights. Say, you don't look so good."

"As though someone hit me on the head and left me for dead?" Margaret said. The irony escaped Spiros.

"It's not safe around here at night," he said, as though saddened by the sorry state of the city.

"I'm all right now," she said. She wondered if she were talking to her attacker. "Is it possible that I pose some sort of threat to you, Spiros?"

"Me? You?" He opened his eyes wide as though shocked at the thought and pressed his large hands to his large chest. "You think I would hit you on the head? Aren't we . . . partners?"

"That remains to be seen," Margaret said.

He eyed her suspiciously. "Just what were you doing on this street anyhow? The people who come here . . ." He stopped.

"I thought I recognized a friend," Margaret said.

Spiros shook his head. "I can't believe you got friends who come around here."

"And just why do *you* happen to be here?"

"Back door to my warehouse. It's easier than unlocking the gate on the front."

It sounded plausible. "Do you know Rebecca Wellington?"

"The name is not familiar." He was not convincing.

"She is a friend who seems to come around here," Margaret said. "So try again." She wondered if the blow to her head had made her exceptionally courageous in this sticky situation. The street was very dark and lonely.

"Oh, *those* Wellingtons. The lawyer. I've had a few dealings with him. Neighborhood business. You know."

"I can believe it," Margaret said. "And his wife?"

"She pursues false dreams, my dear lady. She does not care for me, I think, because I see through her."

"Well, yes. I do have to be going. Suppose you ring me tomorrow as planned, and I'll tell you about my discussions with Castrocani."

She knew he was watching her walk slowly back toward the diner. In spite of the dangers that he implied lurked in the shadows, he had not offered to escort her.

Johnny Mascarpone's name popped into her head as someone whose tastes would run to expensive, low-slung white cars. Carolyn Sue could ferret out that information for her.

Margaret didn't enter the diner but only peered through the glass door. The short-order cook leaned on the counter, reading a Greek newspaper. The waitress she'd seen earlier wasn't there. In her place, a tough-looking youth with a half apron tied around his waist chatted up a couple of lads in leather motorcycle jackets. A couple who looked as though they were testing the waters well beyond the cutting edge of pop fashion sat in a far booth. The male's jewelry was quite eye-catching, if one's taste ran to semisatanic emblems. The female's hair showed the hues of the Italian or perhaps Hungarian flag, depending on which direction one viewed the green, white, and red stripes. Ernie Powers, of the late

Tommy Falco's family, was at the counter, just cutting into a large piece of pie.

Arthur Cramdell was not in evidence, nor was he hovering anywhere on the street nearby.

Margaret returned to her car. The experiences of the evening were beginning to take their toll on her. She noticed that her hands were trembling slightly. The mirror showed a dirty face, and her short, blond hair was in need of a comb. The back of her head still throbbed, and she felt a slight swelling, but there was no blood as far as she could tell.

It did not seem likely that the Arthur Cramdell she had seen at the meeting had hit her over the head, but he could be engaged in some kind of conspiracy, pointing her out to another who followed her when she followed Rebecca. Frances's rumors about him sprang to mind.

Wait a moment, my girl, she thought. Don't succumb to gossip-inspired paranoia. Arthur's apartment was only a block or so away, but she did not feel that she could approach him there, not with Rebecca on the loose.

The two boys in leather came out of the diner and went around to the side. She heard the motorcycle engines start, and seconds later, they appeared on their bikes and roared off.

It occurred to her that Casey Teale was very close, a temporary refuge where she might find two aspirins to case her headache. She didn't choose to walk there, but if there was a parking spot near her apartment, she'd stop. Fate would determine what she would do.

Fate decided that Margaret would stop. There was one rather small space among the closely parked cars that she managed to squeeze into. She rang the downstairs bell and waited. There was no response, but perhaps Casey was in her darkroom. She rang again.

"Are you looking for Casey?" A bearded man with three large Samoyeds at his feet called up to her from the sidewalk. Margaret recognized him as the man who had been concerned about art and life at the meeting.

"Yes. Is she out?" Margaret joined the man on the street.

"She departed very early today." He bowed slightly. The dogs sniffed politely around Margaret's feet. "My name is Jan; I am a neighbor of hers. Did I not see you at the meeting last evening? Lady Margaret, is it?"

"Yes. Where has Casey gone, then?"

He shook his head. "She left me a note saying she'd be out of town for a time, and would I water her plants. I have done this for her when she has had assignments out of town." Jan hesitated. "I saw her on the street after that terrible explosion last night. She was with that odd fellow, Arthur Cramdell. I went to them, and their behavior . . ." The artist shook his head. "She was not herself."

"How so?"

"I believe she was frightened," Jan said. "She loved her art, you know. She said something to the effect that pictures were the cause of it all. I did not understand."

Margaret sat for a moment in her car, with the brown envelope on the seat beside her, and watched Jan and his fierce-looking beasts walk away. "Guy with a dog," one of the girls had said. Surely she would have mentioned it if it had been a pack of dogs. Casey flown, Arthur failing to keep his appointment. Rebecca alone on the dark streets. Spiros looking for his back door. Even Ernie Powers abroad. Where were Sandy and Johnny Mascarpone tonight to round out the group?

She drove toward a wide street that would, she hoped, bring her eventually to the Queens Midtown Tunnel and onto Third Avenue in Manhattan. She had never been so happy to be home.

Chapter 18

Margaret dragged herself awake very early. She knew at a glance in the mirror that she looked terrible. Her face-down fall seemed to have left a small bruise on her cheek. The swelling on the back of her head had subsided, and her headache was fading but was still more than a memory.

She had looked again last night at the photos before taking to her bed. They raised questions her throbbing head did not permit her to answer.

Hoping to catch Arthur before he went to work, she tried to find his number. The operator told her it was unlisted. She would have to hope that he would call her back.

Spiros called promptly on the dot at nine. "How are you feeling this morning, dear lady?"

"Relatively imperfect."

"Ah . . ." Very solicitous today. "How's about I call later?"

"No. What I have to say is briefly said. Mr. Mascarpone is not interested in buying property on the basis you suggested."

"You couldn't have told me this last night? What about that woman? She's the brains."

"I didn't feel well last night," she said. "I can't imagine

how I could present your proposition to Sandy Krofft. Why not do it yourself?''

Spiros was silent.

"Perhaps you have other business dealings with her.''

"She and I may have talked about doing a little business,'' Spiros said. "She wanted me to be her spy around here, back when they were putting the plans for the building together. Then she changed her mind about me. Just give it a try, okay? No names.''

"I don't know that I'll have the opportunity,'' Margaret said.

"You try, we'll talk. You could find me at the warehouse on Saturday.''

"Lots of worry beads coming in, I imagine,'' Margaret said.

"You never know when the ship will dock,'' Spiros said. "Don't forget Nicky's avgolemono. Best egg-lemon soup this side of Salonika.''

It was with faint hope that she would find De Vere that Margaret dialed him at the several numbers where he was sometimes professionally available. On the third try she reached him.

"Has Carolyn Sue upset your household terribly?''

"Not at all,'' he said cheerfully. "I came in very late, and she was safely tucked away. I left very early this morning and caught only the slightest whiff of scent at three hundred dollars an ounce. She must be distressed that the closet space is well filled with Paul's wardrobe, otherwise . . . Is that why you called?''

"Actually, I was wondering if the police got to talk with Casey Teale. Can you find out?''

"I could, but it would take time.'' There was a pause. She knew that De Vere was waiting for her to tell him why she wanted to know.

Finally Margaret said, "Someone I know over there said she'd gone away rather suddenly yesterday morning.''

"I see,'' De Vere said. "I'll try.''

"Thanks,'' she said.

"Are you all right? You sound . . . frail."

"A bit of a headache. I have something I have to do this evening," Margaret said, and did not mention that it had to do with breaking into the offices of Castrocani Development. "Saturday evening is clear. How about you?"

"Clear so far. Oh yes, Carolyn Sue left me a note. Back to Jamaica on the weekend. Ben misses her."

When she thought that Carolyn Sue would be up and about after her fashionable evening on the town, she rang the apartment in Chelsea. It occurred to her that Carolyn Sue was not accustomed to life without willing hands to serve her. Did she even know how to make coffee?

"Were you able to find everything? Coffee or tea?" Margaret asked when Carolyn Sue answered, apparently well into her preparations for the day.

"I'm doin' fine," she said. "I called up those nice boys at the deli down the street, and they ran right over with a cup of coffee."

Willing hands seemed to be available to Carolyn Sue wherever she went. Money helps.

"Oh yes. Delia sent along the office key. The overnight delivery man was here real early. Don't they do a good job?"

"Very good," Margaret said. "I suppose I ought to arrange to meet you at the office, to get a better idea of the lay of the land. I didn't pay much attention on my previous visits."

"Just what would we be lookin' for again?"

Margaret allowed the "we" to pass, although she had no intention of moving fast in the dark with Carolyn Sue at her heels. "Business relationships with the people of Arcadia," she said.

"Let me think," Carolyn Sue said. "I absolutely must have my hair done this morning. The sun in Jamaica has wrecked it. I jes' know every woman at the dinner last night was whisperin' behind her hands about how dreadful I looked, even if I do have a better tan than any of them. Sandy has a meeting with some people—a major tenant who might want to take two floors done up the way they want it. She's good at sweet-talkin' these business fellows.''

"I imagine she's shared with you her vision of what the area will look like.''

"You know, I've never seen the place but once in my life," Carolyn Sue said. She sounded almost wistful. "I'd kinda like a look at it, as long as I'm here. I could call up the limo man I use when I'm in New York and have him drive us over. You could come to the office first and have a private look around. Why, you could take a look at the files then and there.''

"I'd rather do it after hours," Margaret said. "I wouldn't care to have Sandy or Johnny or one of the others see me at it.''

Margaret was about to hang up and see if her own hairdresser had time today to repair the ravages of the previous night, when she remembered to ask, "Carolyn Sue, could you find out what sort of auto Johnny drives? And whether Sandy has a car other than the chauffeured number I saw her in? And where they were last night?''

"Sure! What fun!" Carolyn Sue said.

Margaret wanted to remind her that she was missing the point if she thought murder was fun, but said instead, "Just don't let on why you're asking. Please.''

"Are you goin' to tell *me* why you're askin'?" Carolyn Sue asked. "I got to learn to keep tabs on my employees." Then she added hastily, "I was makin' a joke, Margaret, honey.''

"All will be revealed," Margaret said, and hoped that it would be before someone else was damaged.

Carolyn Sue looked immensely relieved to sink into the ultraluxurious leather seat of the pearl gray limousine she had hired to take her and Margaret to Arcadia in the early afternoon.

"I felt like an intruder in my own company. I've never seen Sandy on such a tear." Carolyn Sue's hair had been refurbished by skillful hands into a floating blond cloud. It would not survive many days back in the Caribbean, but at the moment it was an astonishing thing to behold.

"Sandy wasn't pleased to see me again today," Margaret said. "Although she did ask after De Vere." Taking the opportunity to behave like an especially intrusive colleague of the firm's owner, Margaret had boldly roamed about to fix the layout in her mind: Johnny's office and Sandy's, the office next door for her secretary, two empty offices that Sandy reluctantly stated were for new employees yet to come on board, a small conference room, and a narrow room lined with filing cabinets—apparently unlocked—along with the requisite copier and fax machine. A young woman who said she was an office temporary, in to do some word processing and filing, was sending a lengthy fax.

"Plenty of filing?" Margaret had asked.

Not a lot, apparently, from the temp's response. The lady in charge penciled the names things were to be filed under. She didn't pay much attention, and she preferred offices with more men and more to do. She didn't plan to come back. In the little kitchen, Margaret startled the coffee boy and girl reading magazines and escaped before they pressed a cappuccino on her.

"So few to do so much," Margaret had said to Sandy, who had seemed torn between telling Margaret to mind her own business and the necessity of explaining her operation to an alleged fellow employee.

"I work very hard," Sandy finally said. "And we have support people in the field. The work that requires many hands and more space is handled elsewhere by the project manager's firm and the construction people."

"Perhaps I'll take one of the empty desks for a time," Margaret said, to see how Sandy would react to that possibility. She was rewarded by a brief look of horror.

"Carolyn Sue," Sandy had said then, "I must speak to you. Privately."

"So Sandy took me into that postmodern mess she calls an office and told me that she couldn't work with you hanging about," Carolyn Sue said as the limo entered the Midtown Tunnel, headed for Queens.

"Naturally I wouldn't dream of intentionally spending extended periods in her company," Margaret said. The interior of the limo dimmed in the tunnel, helped along by the densely smoked windows.

"Ma'am . . ." The voice of the driver came to them through an intercom. "I have a report that the expressway is tied up by an accident, so I'm going to take the surface streets."

Carolyn Sue pushed a button and said, "You do what's best." She sat back. "I believe in letting people do the job I pay them for, as long as they do it well." She paused. "I'm beginning to think that maybe Sandy is doin' a different job altogether than the one I hired her to do. She's bein' downright obstructive."

Carolyn Sue was silent for a time, looking at the scene outside the snug comfort of the limo. They passed close to the green Citicorp tower, which looked incongruous rising fifty stories above the low surrounding buildings. Then they left it behind and drove along dingy commercial streets interspersed with orderly residential areas of brick homes built closely together.

"Johnny claims to own one of those fancy Japanese cars," Carolyn Sue said suddenly. "Red. I told him I was gettin' tired of runnin' around Dallas in my Mercedes, since everybody's got one. He was real keen on telling me about his car. Sandy sticks with her car and driver. That's a real expensive proposition, when you think of it." She looked cross now. For all her money, Carolyn Sue was not a careless spendthrift. "I asked him if he were married, and he went into this whole business about bein' single and datin' all these gorgeous women. He started to tell me a story about going out last night with Miss Universe or the like from the way she sounded, but I didn't wait to hear. It sounded like every big lie I ever heard. He's kinda sweet on you, I think. Said you were mighty good-looking for a woman of your age." Margaret looked at her quickly. Carolyn Sue was highly amused.

"And Sandy?"

"Couldn't get a hint," Carolyn Sue said.

"Never mind. We're here. Have your driver go straight ahead for about three blocks and then stop."

Carolyn Sue spoke to the driver, and the car glided to a smooth stop. The driver leapt from his seat and opened the door.

It was a chilly day, slightly overcast. An earth mover in the hole in the ground was lifting up great masses of dirt and rubble and dumping it into a truck. The same muscular young man in the sleeveless padded vest was waving his orange flag at nonexistent traffic. He was delighted to have an opportunity to tell them they couldn't park the limo there.

"I am Principessa Castrocani," Carolyn Sue said grandly, and lifted her chin toward the sign on the fence listing the owner, the general contractor, the architect, the engineers, the interested city agencies, the emergency numbers. All traces of Texas had vanished from her voice, and in its place, a good imitation of a native Italian speaker pronouncing her English words carefully. "It is my building."

The young man thought about that. "I better find the guy who . . ."

"You need find no one," Carolyn Sue said, gracious now. "I am observing the progress. We will soon be gone. I do not believe that my car interrupts the business of digging."

The young man shrugged. The truck was lumbering out of the pit, and he went off to do his job, waving his flag to halt a delivery van that was approaching the exit ramp of the site.

"You did that well," Margaret said.

"Ah may not be real good at *readin'* Italian," Carolyn Sue said, once again the duly crowned queen of Texas, "all those negatives and tenses and things, but I sure could talk the lingo when I wanted to. Margaret, honey? You still with me?"

"Sorry. I had a thought." Margaret was wondering whether Prince Aldo in faraway Italy had actually written that Johnny Mascarpone was a long-lost Castrocani cousin;

or had he written something quite different? "Shall we walk about a bit? There's not much to see here at the site."

Margaret guided Carolyn Sue toward the newly demolished building. The sidewalk in front was still cordoned off with orange crime scene tape. Two official-looking men were carefully examining the rubble. The surviving buildings on either side had been shored up with new lumber.

"Those are the buildings Sandy says have got to come down as soon as the police let us get on with it," Carolyn Sue said. "Too dangerous to let them stand. Now, let me get this straight. That poor woman was killed over there, and the man at the old buildings?"

"Yes," Margaret said slowly. She was recalling the night of the explosion, the lights and the crowds, Father Steve pushing his way through the people to Tommy, Casey with her camera raised. "Carolyn Sue, if you are willing to take a walk, there's someone I'd like you to meet."

Carolyn Sue's boots had sinfully high heels, but she said bravely, "Sure, honey. I'm good for a mile at least."

Margaret led her past the diner, which had become her landmark in the neighborhood, and along a street where the stumpy spire of Saint Lucy's stood out above the nearby buildings.

Now that the snow had vanished, the flower beds circling the statue of Saint Lucy showed a few dry stalks from last year's geraniums. A notice board listing mass and confession times stood beside the statue. Margaret led Carolyn Sue up the concrete walk to the church door and tried the round brass knob.

"What are we doin' here?" Carolyn Sue whispered in deference to the religious setting as the door opened smoothly.

"I'm hoping the priest will be about. I'd like to speak to him."

Carolyn Sue gazed down the darkened nave toward the altar. A few candles in red glass holders flickered before statues of saints in niches on either side, and a little light filtered in through the stained-glass windows.

"I used to go into all these churches back in Italy," Carolyn Sue said. "Seemed the most natural thing in the world, but since I got back to Texas, I don't believe I've set foot in a Catholic church. This is quite . . . plain."

"You're missing the baroque Bernini touches. Ah, Father Steve . . ."

He was standing near a confessional reading a small book. "Who . . . ? Lady Margaret. You startled me. Very few people come to the church on weekday afternoons."

"Father Steve, this is Carolyn Sue Hoopes."

"Not the devil in human form," Carolyn Sue said, "although some of your parishioners might not agree."

He grinned. "I'm glad to meet you, and I wouldn't be saying that to the devil."

"You know, the Holy Father said something to that effect to me. John Twenty-three. Lovely man. It was when I was living in Rome, even before my son, Paul, was born." Carolyn Sue stopped. It must have occurred to her that it was also probably before the priest was born. "Quite a long time ago."

Father Steve chuckled. "I do know of him, and Rome is a wonderful city, isn't it?"

"We don't want to take you away from your work," Margaret said quickly, lest Carolyn Sue indulge in extended reminiscences of her days as a Roman princess. "I'd like to speak to you alone for a moment."

Father Steve tilted his head toward the far aisle. Carolyn Sue chose to gaze toward the round window above the altar while Margaret and Father Steve retreated to a statue with an unusually large number of lighted candles before it.

"Saint Jude," he said. "Hopeless causes. He's especially popular these days." He turned to her and looked her in the eye. "What is it you wish to ask me, Lady Margaret?"

"You were summoned the other night when Tommy Falco was found at the explosion. I saw you there and am now wondering how you knew to come so quickly."

"As I understand it, a message was brought. I don't know by whom. I was in the back room at the parish hall turning down the thermostat. You can't imagine how expensive heating oil is, and our janitor had gone home. Peter Wellington found me, told me that someone came with word that a man was dying near those old, boarded-up buildings, and that I was needed. He went off to see about the explosion, and I followed close on his heels. Tommy had been dead for a while, the police said. He wasn't much of a churchgoer himself, but his family . . . Mrs. Powers . . .''

"Thank you, Father. My curiosity is satisfied. I say, Mrs. Hoopes has a charitable heart; she's feeling a bit guilty about her impact on Arcadia, and of course, she's very rich. . . .''

"Charity is a great blessing,'' Father Steve said solemnly, but there was a twinkle in his lovely blue eyes.

"Mrs. Hoopes,'' he said as they rejoined Carolyn Sue, who was still striving to look spiritual and succeeding quite well in spite of her designer labels. Margaret could easily imagine her charming the pope, although certainly not taking him in. "I'm afraid we don't compare with your great Roman churches, but we do serve our parishioners as best we can, providing the rain doesn't come through the roof.''

"I do know about leaky roofs,'' she said. "Terrible for the wood.''

"It's been a pleasure to meet you,'' Father Steve said.

"Father Steve, honey, if there's any little thing I can ever do . . .''

His eyes flickered mischievously toward Margaret and back to Carolyn Sue. "Yes, there is. I'd like very much, very much indeed, to be allowed to offer a blessing at the official opening of your building. Aside from my interest in good community feeling, it might be an excellent public relations gesture for you.''

"Margaret, you fox. That's why you brought me round. Public relations at work! Father Steve, you can take it as carved in stone that you'll do the honors. And about this leaking roofs of yours. I'd be right pleased to contribute to your roof fund. If you don't have one, you should. Every church I know of has one, just in case it's needed.'' Carolyn Sue beamed benignly at him, and Margaret and Father Steve exchanged another look. Carolyn Sue had the wisdom of the very rich when it came to subtle pleas for charity. She was clearly miles ahead of amateurs like the priest and Margaret.

"Such a diplomat," Carolyn Sue said as they emerged into weak sunshine. "Did you find out what you wanted to know?"

"I know something," Margaret said, "but I'm not entirely sure what it means. Have you seen enough?"

"I got a good fix on the place. My building isn't going to make it much prettier, but it's not going to make it worse."

"But is this one building the end?"

"Now that remains to be seen. I don't know what's lying ahead."

Margaret was leading them back to the limo by way of the street where Casey lived. She thought she might try to ring her bell in case she was back. To her surprise, when she rang, a buzzer sounded, and she was able to open the front door.

"I just want to speak to a friend," Margaret said.

"Who is there?"

Margaret recognized the voice. "Jan? It's Lady Margaret."

"Ah. I am doing the plants. Casey isn't back."

"Could I show a visitor Casey's photos? We won't stay long."

"Well, I . . . All right. Come up."

Carolyn Sue followed Margaret up the stairs to Casey's bare white apartment.

"This will be a view of the neighborhood you can't get by walking about," Margaret said.

Jan was standing at the door with a polished brass watering can with a long spout. Behind him on the rugless, polished floor, his three blue-eyed dogs sat in a row, restrained by invisible bonds of obedience. One tail thumped on the floor at the sight of visitors.

"Jan, this is Mrs. Benton Hoopes."

Jan examined Carolyn Sue's well-groomed splendor. He seemed to approve.

"Please enjoy Casey's art. The dogs will not trouble you.

Casey is very good, I think. My work, of course, is in a different medium.''

"Oh, I could jes' tell by *lookin'* at you that you are an artist," Carolyn Sue said. "There's some kind of aura around true artists. I'm very sensitive that way. . . ."

Carolyn Sue's nonsense was gratefully accepted, and she walked over to the wall of photos, pausing to place a gentle hand on the muzzle of one of the dogs. Three tails thumped. Carolyn Sue could probably entrance a grizzly.

Carolyn Sue examined the black-and-white photos closely, seeing for the first time the people of the neighborhood and the setting for their lives. Margaret followed her and saw faces and places that had become familiar to her.

"I do believe that's Johnny," Carolyn Sue murmured. "Looks mighty furtive to me, as though he's doin' a drug buy. Who's this?''

Frances Rassell posed stiffly in front of a nicely kept row house with a short flight of steps leading up to the front door. The photo was similar to the one Margaret had gotten from Alice, but it was somehow more revealing: sharp and suspicious. No wonder Frances had spoken of ''the ugly truth.''

"This is Frances Rassell," Margaret said.

"I see." Carolyn Sue moved on.

There was Ernie Powers leaning on the bonnet of a car and talking across it to a defeated-looking Tommy Falco. Rebecca Wellington got up in sequined splendor for a night out, followed out of the house by a tuxedoed Peter. Several shots of Jan and his dogs. Frances gossiping with the large woman Margaret thought was Ernie's wife. She paused before a shot of a single figure walking at dusk down one of the blank warehouse streets lined with parked cars. Again it was similar to one that Frances had, but here it was clearly Rebecca Wellington. Far down the street parked among the other cars was a low white sports car.

"These are real fine," Carolyn Sue said. She indicated a series of architectural shots, sharp black-and-white photos of bits of buildings, cornices, worn steps, wrought-iron fences delicately topped with snow, a wall of graffiti. Then came photos of men starting to dig into a rubble-strewn lot that stretched into the distance. The hole began and deepened in succeeding pictures. Trucks and construction workers. Tommy watching from the sidelines.

Margaret was thoughtful. "You've heard nothing from Casey?" she asked Jan, who had finished watering the spider plants.

"She is an independent lady. She could be anywhere—the Arizona desert, Europe, Manhattan. . . ."

"If she returns soon, please ask her to ring me," Margaret said. "And tell her to be careful."

Jan was taken aback. "Is she in danger, then?"

"Yes," Margaret said. "I believe she is."

When Margaret and Carolyn Sue were again safely ensconced in the limousine and heading back to Manhattan, Margaret said, "What do you think?"

"It's not exactly as I imagined it," Carolyn Sue said. "You kinda forget about the people when you're lookin' at engineering blueprints and architecturals. Well, it's too late to regret tearing the place apart, but I'll see what I can do to make it less painful."

"That's going to mean a struggle with Sandy," Margaret said. "I think she has a vision. . . ."

"Don't you worry about her," Carolyn Sue said. "She works for me, not the other way around."

Chapter 19

*M*argaret *did* not favor the idea of taking Carolyn Sue with her to visit the Castrocani offices after hours but could not dissuade her from coming.

"You got to sign in downstairs; there's a guard. Who has a better right there than me? It will save trouble in the long run. I won't bother you."

Margaret finally saw her point. She would hate to be in the middle of her inspection of the files only to come face-to-face with a curious security guard. With Carolyn Sue on hand, however, Margaret was not an obvious trespasser.

"Then what time will I be pickin' you up?"

"Early. Seven-thirty," Margaret said. Carolyn Sue looked disappointed that it was not to be a stealthy midnight visit.

With Carolyn Sue off to don a black cat suit, worn no doubt with a simple strand of pearls in order to burglarize her own property in suitable style, Margaret placed a call to the Caribbean.

"Margaret! What has my mother done now?" Paul's concern was touching. "She has been known to try on garments in the shops and leave, forgetting she has not taken them off." The thought of Carolyn Sue absentmindedly absconding with a five-thousand-dollar Romeo Gigli beaded vest was worth contemplating.

"Everything is fine," Margaret said. "Almost. Do be a love and ring your father in Italy. He's on the telephone, isn't he?"

"Yes, such as the system is there, but I learn that he is spending the winter in Monte Carlo as the guest of one of those prosperous Eastern European tennis stars. I need not worry that he will lose the family fortune at the casino, as there is no fortune to lose. What do you wish to know?"

"I should like to know the true relationship of one John Mascarpone to the Famiglia Castrocani. John claims to be related."

"*Principessa* has mentioned him, but I have never heard my father speak of the family. I can try to reach Papa now and ring you back. If not, I'll try tomorrow in the late afternoon, as we will be scuba diving most of the day."

"Excellent," Margaret said. "I understand that Carolyn Sue is flying back to you in a day or two."

"She will be welcome," Paul said. "Ben, in his loneliness, is paying far too much attention to a delectable beauty a third his age. I saw her first, but as he is far richer than I. . . . Margaret, this holiday has done great things for me. It is like the old days when I was allowed to roam the continent without a thought of how much it was costing my mother." Paul firmly believed that he was intended to lead his life with no less than five stars next to all accommodations, dining spots, vehicles, and purveyors of fine gentlemen's clothing he encountered.

"Have you found the murderer yet?" he added before hanging up.

"You know that is not the business I am involved in with your mother."

"How odd. Her very last words before she boarded the Gulfstream, which flew her to New York, were that you had promised to solve the crime."

"I made no such promise, but I am beginning to have an idea."

"Take care," Paul said. "Does De Vere know what you are doing?"

"I am merely thinking, not doing." But, of course, this was not true. She was preparing to don casual clothes, tasteful, neither showy nor sinister, readying herself to uncover the business behind the business at Castrocani Development.

She left her apartment disappointed that Arthur Cramdell hadn't left a message on her machine, but more likely than not, he would be one of the "nicer" people of the neighborhood Rebecca would invite to her brunch. She was looking forward to Sunday with more than a little interest.

The gray limo was at her door at seven-thirty on the dot. When Margaret and Carolyn Sue arrived at the office building, it was simple for Carolyn Sue to sign her name in the guard's book, and Margaret's below it, both quite illegible.

Sandy Krofft ran an orderly operation. The horizontal file drawers showed color-coded folders, with the letters and documents arranged chronologically in each.

"What sort of business does Sandy have that I don't know about?" Carolyn Sue asked. "There's not an awful lot of stuff in these files."

"Perhaps she's counting on a rapid expansion," Margaret said. "Ah. Wellington."

"I'll leave you to it," Carolyn Sue said, and wandered off to peer into the silent offices and perhaps to contemplate the portrait of the old cardinal in the reception area.

The Wellington file contained a lengthy proposal from Rebecca about representing the public relations interests of the new building. It looked very detailed, and the fees seemed very high. The cover letter indicated that Rebecca would be willing, nay, eager, to consider handling the project on her own rather than through her firm. It didn't seem entirely ethical to Margaret, but she understood that many people in New York in all areas of endeavor were capable of cutting ethical corners if the money was right. A formal letter from Sandy acknowledged receipt. She was surprised to find a badly typed letter from Peter Wellington, dated a few days earlier. He must have written it without benefit of secretary:

> *Dear Sandy, I tried to reach you by phone but couldn't, so I'm messengering this over right away. I know she has submitted her proposal, but don't fall for it, even if you think you would be doing me a favor. You wouldn't be, and you wouldn't be helping Castrocani—or us, which is more important. She has a lot more problems than we thought.*
> *Always, Peter.*

There was some formal correspondence from several months before to and from Peter Wellington, relating to the Arcadia Neighborhood Action Committee. Margaret noticed that "Dear Miss Krofft" and "Dear Mr. Wellington" eventually turned into "Dear Sandy" and "Dear Peter," but none of the contents were in the least suspicious.

At the back of the folder, Margaret came across another bit of paper: a handwritten note saying,

> *Miss Krofft, I won't be put off. I have got to see you. I know what's going on now, and I will show you how I know. You could stop by the next time you're here, or I could come to the city.*

It was signed *F. Russell*.

The writing was labored, careful.

Why was this note here? A penciled note on the top said *File Wellington*, so there had been no filing error.

Margaret looked under *R*, but there was no Rassell file. She glanced quickly through the rest of the drawer containing the end of the alphabet. No familiar names. No Spiros, although that certainly was his given name rather than a family name. Nothing remotely Greek caught her eye.

She looked in vain for a file labeled *Sandlot*. It occurred to her that the information she sought might well be stored in one of the computers around the office without hard copies in the files, but she wasn't prepared to search the floppy disks.

She decided to start at the beginning of the alphabet.

Her reward—under *A* was a thick hanging file labeled *Arcadia*. In it were individual red, green, blue, and manila folders labeled with names that seemed to cover the range of people she'd met.

"Margaret, honey, you findin' anything of interest?"

"I believe I have, Carolyn Sue, but I'm not sure yet."

"Well, then. Do you suppose this is somethin'?" Carolyn Sue handed her a sheet of paper, a street plan that looked like Arcadia. The new building was clearly indicated in black. Around it were a number of spaces also marked in black, along with many spaces colored red and a few left unmarked. Farther away from the new building, both the red patches and the black were fewer, with more white spaces.

"Where did you find this?"

"On the secretary's desk, just lyin' there. Oh, don't worry, there was a pile of them, all the same. Nobody's goin' to miss one, and I suppose I have a right to take away one if I want."

"It appears to show the buildings in the neighborhood, indicating something. . . . Look. That row of three houses I know is Castrocani property—it's where the explosion occurred. It has the same markings as the new building, so black must mean Castrocani. I judge the blank spaces are uncommitted, and the red ones could mean parcels that are on the market, or ones that your company has approached. . . ."

Carolyn Sue was frowning. "I had in mind to build a few satellite buildings around the big one. That multiplex movie thing and a sort of mini-mall of shops for the apartments and the office workers. They're going to want what they're used to if we're to keep them happy."

"No hotels, low-rise garden apartments, high-rise apartments, planned community sort of thing?"

"That's not what I had in mind. Real estate is kinda risky these days."

Margaret looked through the files. "Someone has a different idea," she said, "and I think this plan says what it is. Johnny mentioned it: a big project that will overshadow yours. I think that other interests are buying up the property. The parcels marked in red." She started to leaf through the file. "Look."

It was not difficult to figure out that Persons A, B, and C had sold property in the Arcadia section to Persons D, E, and F, who had thereupon resold it to a company called Sandlot. It appeared that S. Agoras, F. Rassell, and Guido Mascarpone had profited handsomely in their dealings with Sandlot. Margaret knew she was looking at the bare bones of the transactions; the meat was doubtless elsewhere.

"I think," Margaret said, "that your trusted Sandy Krofft has been developing a parallel operation. 'Sandlot' for Sandy Krofft. I don't think she was going to propose that you expand rather more widely than you've planned and be in a position to sell her holdings to Castrocani."

"You think she was expecting to expand on her own." Carolyn Sue looked mightily put out. "Where do you suppose she got the money? Banks aren't lending on the basis of a pretty face or anything else these days."

"She may have built up a backlog of favors owed. Maybe she has partners."

"Maybe she's been siphoning off some of our operating money. Maybe I should have someone check to be sure the old cardinal's portrait out there is still the real thing."

"This is pure speculation, Carolyn Sue. Still, all those people . . . It might explain the vandalism in the neighborhood to help people decide to sell; but why kill Frances Rassell?"

"She was goin' to expose Sandy?"

"I'm not convinced of that." She wished she could talk to Arthur Cramdell. He knew something about what had been going on. He'd talked to Casey, and Casey was frightened.

Something was missing, Margaret knew. Even if Frances knew all about Sandy's covert plans, even if Frances had decided from the picture of Sandy and Peter Wellington that something scandalous was going on between them . . .

Carolyn Sue was getting restless.

"Expose someone," Margaret said. "Of course. Carolyn Sue, could you amuse yourself for a few minutes more?"

"I could." Carolyn Sue was almost sullen. "Except I'll just be thinkin' about how I've been betrayed. This sure is making me hungry," Carolyn Sue said, "but I'm not dressed to be seen anywhere decent."

"We'll go to my flat," Margaret said, "and get Chinese takeout delivered. First I want to see if I can ferret out names of people who might be involved in all these property sales. The real estate broker, money people—all possibly entirely unaware of Sandy's double activities. The files aren't extensive, and if I don't find anything right away, we'll leave." She found the switch that turned the copier on and waited until it was ready. She copied a couple of pages about Sandlot's acquisitions. Then she found the Wellington file to copy Peter's note and the note from Frances. She glanced again at the formal letters between Peter and Sandy, hers on Castrocani stationery, his on his law firm's.

She stopped and gazed up at the tasteful modern lighting fixtures over her head shedding an economical fluorescent glow on the room.

"Yes," she said out loud. "Frances meant to expose someone."

Before turning out the lights, she surveyed the file room. No evidence of their visit. She was feeling better, now that she had a solid idea about what all this business in Arcadia might mean.

"Aren't you leaving for Jamaica any moment now?" she asked Carolyn Sue as they rode down to the lobby in the elevator.

"I was, but until this is settled . . ."

Margaret debated telling her about Ben's solution to lone-liness and decided to mind her own business.

Paul had sent a fax while she was out:

Tell *carissima mama mia* that Vito Mascarpone was Grandfather's servant. He spent his early years at the villa trying to keep it from falling down. He was in the army during the Second World War, and after it, he took his brother Guido, his wife, and his son Gianni to America. They are not members of our family. *Princĭpessa*'s un-derstanding of Italian negatives has never been good. It is, I think, because she does not like to hear the word "no."

Carolyn Sue looked chagrined when she read the fax. "I had no idea. . . . I knew I should have taken Aldo's letter to the nice Italian maître d' at that restaurant we go to all the time in Dallas."

"It's too late to worry," Margaret said. "The family did well. Johnny said his father and his uncle were in construction."

"Well, I've got to do something about him—as well as her, don't I?"

"I should think so, but I'd wait a day or two, speaking as your public relations expert."

A breathless Chinese waiter arrived at Margaret's door with rather too much food.

"I do like a nice scallion pancake," Carolyn Sue said. "And tangerine chicken. Is this lobster in black bean sauce?" She seemed more content now. "Margaret, aren't you going to try any of this?"

The buzzer sounded from downstairs.

"Who could that be? Didn't I pay the delivery man the right amount?"

"Gentleman to see you, Lady Margaret," the doorman said. "Doesn't want to give a name, says he's a friend, and asks if you could come down to the lobby."

"What does he look like?"

"Ordinary," the doorman said. "Not dangerous. I'll watch out for you if you come down."

"What is it now?" Carolyn Sue asked. A woman of many parts, she was handling chopsticks with ease.

"I must go down to the lobby for a moment," Margaret said. "Save some of the lobster for me."

The lobby of Margaret's high rise was stiffly formal, with big mirrors, potted plants, and a frequently polished marble floor. A few uncomfortable chairs and sofas did not encourage hanging around.

"He stepped outside," the doorman said. "Seemed kind of nervous."

"A big man with a mustache, perhaps?"

The doorman shook his head. "There he is, out there in the shadows. You bring him inside or stand right in front of the door where I can see you."

"You're better than a bodyguard, Gerry," Margaret said. She ventured cautiously outside. "Arthur!"

Arthur Cramdell started at the sound of her voice.

"I tried to meet you last night," she said. "I . . . I had an accident."

"I didn't come. I apologize. I started out but . . . I was afraid."

"Why, Arthur?"

"Casey told me something after the meeting. I ran into her near where Tommy Falco was killed."

"She's gone away," Margaret said. "She was afraid, too."

He took a deep breath. "She told me about Tommy saying that somebody was going to pay him off to keep quiet about seeing Frances's murder."

"I know about that," Margaret said.

"Then I told Casey that I'd seen Tommy coming out of the Wellingtons' house that morning. She said there were dangerous things going on, and she didn't want to get mixed up in them. She told me to be careful."

"I see. How well do you know Rebecca and Peter?"

"Not too well. She doesn't like me. She has some lofty idea that she's better than everyone else, meant for better things. You know the type. I met Peter through the real estate company I work for.''

"I see. I suppose you know all about real estate.''

"I just do word processing, but . . .''

"Then answer one question before you leave, about what sort of people act as brokers for buying and selling property." She nodded as he explained.

Arthur Cramdell walked down the block, shoulders hunched. Margaret hoped he would take her advice and make himself scarce around the neighborhood for a time. He had friends in Manhattan, he said, with whom he could stay if he decided to get away for a few days.

Carolyn Sue had put the remains of the Chinese food in the oven to stay warm and was leafing through *Vanity Fair*. "I tell you, Margaret, Calvin Klein has got to be stopped, but it's a job for a better woman than me. Something wrong?''

"Nothing to concern you," she said. "A friend had some information for me. I say, I'm going around to Dianne Stark's place tomorrow afternoon to help address some envelopes for this charity business. Would you like to join us? Dianne would love to see you.''

"I don't know that I could be my usual charmin' self with all these problems. I might go off and buy myself a trinket to cheer me up. And I'll see about flights back to Jamaica and maybe give Ben a call." She grinned. "I suppose he's chasin' after those cute little things in their bikinis. Unlike Aldo, Ben just looks and spends a little money on 'em.''

"Shall I see you before you leave?" Margaret asked. "I have that brunch at the Wellingtons' on Sunday, but I won't stay long. Just long enough to see what Rebecca and Peter have to say for themselves in the midst of their friends.''

Carolyn Sue was thoughtful. "I won't be leavin' town before Monday, I think. I got a little more business to straighten out. You call me tomorrow. I'll be at the apartment—or maybe the office.''

"Oh?"

"I took a look at the place," Carolyn Sue said, "and decided it could do with some redecorating."

Chapter 20

Saturday morning felt like a reprieve for Margaret: there was nothing she could do about her suspicions except to look again at Casey's pictures to try to trace the stories they might conceal and to review the papers she had copied and the plan with its red markings.

The glossy images told a tale of clandestine meetings: Rebecca with an unknown person on an unfrequented street, Peter with Sandy, Spiros, and Peter. And Casey, who had seen it all, since she had taken the pictures, and she was gone.

The brunch tomorrow would at least give Margaret the opportunity to ask diplomatic questions and possibly find connections. That settled, Saturday morning could now be devoted to doing often-postponed exercises and changing the cable television channels frequently to see what strange electronic marvels were speeding out into space to entertain other worlds. She paused at the channel dedicated to Indian programming. An exuberant couple was singing and dancing against a background of an ornate but decaying palace. She wondered if it could belong to her old friend the Maharajah of Tharpur.

The weekly cleaning lady, who had failed to appear on the day before, arrived just before noon.

"I couldn't come yesterday," Altagracia said. "Luis was . . ."

Margaret raised her hand to silence her. She did not want to hear what Altagracia's son was up to now. She had heard too many stories of his close encounters with the forces of law and order to want to know the latest chapter.

Altagracia said, "These drugs, these friends of his. He dreams false dreams." Altagracia had once worked for a psychiatrist and fancied herself an expert analyst. "You going to be staying around while I'm here?"

"What? No. I'll be going out shortly."

"Some kind of fish die in here?" Altagracia regarded the neatly tied bag of trash Margaret had not yet taken to the trash chute. It contained, she knew, a few fragments of lobster shell.

"I had some people in," Margaret said. Priam's Priory butlers did not discuss the contents of the trash, but things were different in America. "Just take care of everything. Thanks so much."

For Dianne Stark's gathering of the ladies with a charitable bent, Margaret donned a pink silk shirt and tailored beige trousers with matching suede boots. She examined her face and thought that the bruise from her encounter two nights before was scarcely noticeable. The vacuum cleaner roared to life as she departed with the hope that Altagracia would see her way to doing a bit of dusting.

"Hello, hello!" Dianne looked more fecund than even two days before. "They're all here, chewing up their absent friends at a great rate." Margaret could hear high-pitched chatter from the small sitting room off the entrance hall of the Starks' huge apartment. "You didn't bring Carolyn Sue, I see. Dorothy was at dinner with her the other night. Said she looked marvelous."

"She decided she had too much on her mind. I believe she intends to try a new stress-reduction technique involving the inspection of unset diamonds with a borrowed loupe."

As Margaret followed Dianne into the tastefully pastel

room with a half-dozen chattering ladies and one man sitting at little tables, pens in hand, she heard a terribly refined voice say, "So when my husband saw the bills, I explained that all this shopping was *not* my fault. It's because of all this easy credit. . . ."

"Here's Margaret," someone said. "Sit here by me, darling. Some of the oddest people are getting invitations. Does anybody know a Doctor Emil Glass?"

Margaret touched checks with the woman. "I do know him, Pauline. He's a dentist who likes charity parties. Hullo, Sophia, Nancy. Bitsy's here, too. And Dorothy. And Harry . . . Please don't try to get up out of that chair, Harry. You'll spoil the lovely drape of your trousers."

Harry Dowd sat back down in the overstuffed chair he had no doubt chosen because it put him in the center of the group.

"I barely had a word with you the other night," he said. "We must have lunch. How's that brother of yours?"

"The young earl is thriving, complete with devoted fiancée. This one looks like a sure bet to become the new Countess of Brayfield."

"Here's a list of addresses, Margaret," Dianne said. "Here are the envelopes. We're trying to be elegant and neat in our handwriting, but some of us have forgotten our penmanship drills, including me. Give Margaret some space, Pauline. There."

"Didn't Poppy Dill tell me you were solving a murder?" someone asked. "For Carolyn Sue?"

"I had dinner on Thursday with Carolyn Sue and a few others at Don and Ruth Ames's place," Dorothy said. "She flew up from Jamaica. . . ."

"We can't bear Jamaica," Bitsy said. "Lyford Cay for us, every year. Did I tell you about the to-do there in January with Halliday Monckton and that tart he travels with?"

Margaret bent over her pile of envelopes and smiled to herself. The tide of gossip had erased the comment about murder from their minds.

"You must remember the tales about Monckton's second wife—no, Gladys was his third," Harry Dowd said. "She's the one who had the affair with the eighteen-year-old *and* that fat old baron at the same time. Monckton found out about them both on the same day.'' All hands ceased to write, and all eyes were on the slight, dapper Harry with his slightly touched-up light brown hair and the devotedly cared-for baby-smooth skin. The tiny cosmetic surgery scars were visible only in the worst lighting. "You *must* have heard this. Poppy knows the absolutely true story, and she told me in *strictest* confidence."

"What now?" Dianne said. The doorbell had sounded far away in the apartment. "The maid will get it. Go on about Gladys, Harry. I had her on a flight years ago. A perfect demon." Dianne was not the least self-conscious about her former career as a flight attendant.

The maid appeared at the door.

"Yes, Rose?" Dianne said.

"A lady to see you, ma'am. A Mrs. . . ."

"Dianne! I hope I'm not too terribly late." A resplendent Rebecca Wellington brushed past the maid into the room. "I must have forgotten to write the time on my calendar. I was just at the office clearing up a few matters and noticed that Ned Griscom had a note about today. . . ."

The eyes that had been fastened on Harry in heated anticipation of a scandalous tale were now directed in icy union toward Rebecca.

"Mrs. Wellington," Dianne said, "there was no need to come. I told Mr. Griscom that my committee people could handle the addressing. But please do join us. Do you know everyone?"

"Of course! Hello, Harry darling. And dear Margaret." The chill in the room deepened sufficiently to frost silver mint julep cups. Rebecca seemed not to notice. There was a certain desperation in her sparkly smile. Although she was dressed to kill in a soft wool A-line dress of deep plum with matching hose and ankle-high boots with fur trim, Margaret thought she looked unwell, with circles under her eyes that the most expensive foundation makeup could not erase.

"Can I have Rose bring you tea or something?" Dianne said.

"Don't trouble, Dianne. I'll just squeeze in here beside Margaret and . . ."

"Mrs. Benedict," Dorothy said in her tightest grande dame voice. "I do not believe we have met."

"But, Dorothy, we have! At the reception. Harry darling, we must reschedule to have drinks sometime soon."

"Yes, well. I'll call you," Harry said.

Dianne caught Margaret's eye and tilted her head toward the door almost imperceptibly.

"Look at the time," Margaret said. "I should make a phone call, Dianne."

"Of course. Charlie's study. I'll show you the way."

"I ought to . . . I'll just go out with you," Harry Dowd said. "Mrs. Wellington can take up where I left off on my list. I won't be but a minute."

As the door to the sitting room closed behind them, Dianne said, "What in the world possessed her to show up? I made it absolutely clear to her firm that we would take care of addressing the invitations."

" 'Harry darling,' she called me," Harry said. "I scarcely know the woman. I was toying with the idea of having a public relations person for about one second but changed my mind." He almost pouted. "The engagement to meet for drinks was never definite, although she makes it sound as though we're regular chums."

"I certainly can't throw her out," Dianne said, "but she's put a damper on . . . the easy flow of conversation."

"Overstimulated," Harry said. "I recognize the signs. Beverly what's-it—the one who died of an overdose . . ."

"The powder room is that way, Harry," Dianne said.

Dianne drew Margaret into Charlie's comfortable study, all masculine leather and wood and beautifully bound books. She sank into an enormous armchair and sighed. "Why is this Wellington woman doing this to me? It's hard enough for *me* to be 'one of us.' You know what those women in there are like. It's beyond imagining that she will ever be.

And this performance surely is no way to make a run at breaking into the charmed circle.''

"She's looking for a cushion," Margaret said, "to ease a long, long fall.''

"Whatever does that mean?"

"The future is not bright for Mrs. Wellington," Margaret said.

When Margaret and Dianne returned to the silent sitting room, the ladies were rapidly addressing envelopes and attending not at all to their penmanship. The voices of gossip had been stilled.

"That's my list done," Harry Dowd said suddenly. "Must be off. Lovely afternoon, Dianne. Ladies, who'll be at Mortimer's on Tuesday? Not you, Dorothy?"

"I'm off to Palm Beach on Monday," she said. "Just for the week. But perhaps," she added wickedly, "Mrs. Wellington will be allowed a long lunch hour."

Rebecca started. "No. No, I'm not free," she said. "I'll be out of town myself."

Margaret thought Rebecca looked as though the cushion was not as soft and comforting as she had expected. "I ought to be leaving, too. So much to do . . ."

At Dianne's urging, Margaret did not leave with the others. Rebecca had hung back so as not to ride down in the elevator with Harry and the women. Margaret spoke to her at the door. "I'll be seeing you tomorrow, then?"

"Yes, tomorrow," Rebecca said. She looked on the brink of tears. "I'm afraid I haven't had time to . . . You're sure you want to come?"

"Absolutely," Margaret said. She hoped Rebecca didn't think that she would behave as cruelly as the committee ladies.

"How awful those witches can be," Dianne said when she and Margaret were alone. "I'm probably no better, but I do have the excuse that she's been shamelessly coquettish toward my husband. One has to protect one's turf."

"One does," Margaret said. "Poor Rebecca seems desperate to share in the alleged glamour of our little social

world. Doesn't like being the hired man around the estate."
But Margaret knew that wasn't the whole story. She did not
say to Dianne that she was now fairly convinced that Rebecca's husband was involved with murder as well as an elaborate scheme to outwit, if not defraud, Carolyn Sue. She did
not say that Rebecca must know that her life as she knew it—
and as she dreamed it might be—was, sooner or later, going
to be much altered.

Chapter 21

Whatever her suspicions of Peter Wellington's role in the deaths in Arcadia, Margaret did not think that he posed a serious danger to her in the midst of people tucking into scrambled eggs with a sprinkling of lower grade caviar, hot croissants, and pitchers of mimosas and Bloody Marys.

She certainly did not mention the murders, the attack on her, or her plans to go across the river once more when she met De Vere on Saturday evening.

He did mention the case in passing. "Your friend the photographer did not speak with the police," he said. "They are interested in locating her." He looked at her expectantly.

"No idea where she is, really," Margaret said. "I'm sure she's all right."

"They also want to speak with that odd man who addressed the meeting. Arthur Cramdell," he said. "He's gone missing, too."

"No! I just spoke . . . That is, he said he was staying with friends."

"Margaret," De Vere said warningly.

"He came around to speak with me," she said defensively. "About the neighborhood." It would do no good, she thought, to attempt to explain and possibly spoil their evening. Arthur would tell what he knew to the right people, and they would sort it out. So she kept silent and even put her upcoming social engagement in Queens out of her mind.

"Anyhow," De Vere said, "they're beginning to come around again to the idea of muggers on the loose. Lots of drug activity over there recently."

"I see," Margaret said. They went far downtown to a Provençal restaurant that was half as good as the review she'd read but twice as good as she expected.

Sunday morning was overcast, but the day was not cold, and the hints of spring were growing stronger.

"Hasn't been so bad a winter after all," the taxi driver who dropped her in front of the Wellingtons' house said. "But you always got to look out for the March blizzard."

There were many empty parking spaces on the street, and no one was abroad except for a man hurrying along with a thick Sunday *New York Times* under his arm.

Margaret was curious to see how the people of the neighborhood—the "nicer" ones—related in a purely social setting, with no tempers raised by debate and no distant sound of giant earth movers to remind them that Carolyn Sue would be with them in spirit and concrete and glass for years to come.

As she was dressing, she had decided that she would take Peter aside and suggest that, as a lawyer, he ought to find a really good lawyer for himself. She had no proof that he was directly involved with Frances's death, but his relationship with Sandy, for whom apparently nothing held any terrors, made it likely that he must have thought that she had pulled the strings that ended in murder. Maybe she would go so far as to hint that she was aware that Rebecca perhaps had problems with controlled substances. Then she had remembered the pain of the blow to her head: Rather than someone who resented her role as a representative of the building, could it have been someone specifically deflecting her from her pursuit of Rebecca?

With that thought in mind, she looked up at the Wellington house. It was pleasant enough, with wrought-iron gratings on the street-level windows, painted trim, a new-looking door. The tall windows on the floor above showed a white ceiling, with louvered shutters in natural wood on the lower half of the windows, slightly open. She thought she saw someone draw back as she examined the house. The top floor windows, presumably Arthur's apartment, had lowered venetian blinds.

It was ten minutes past one. Margaret rang the bell.

It was quite a long minute before Rebecca opened the door. Margaret was startled to see how dreadful she looked: pale and tired with pronounced dark circles under her eyes. Her hair was drawn back behind her ears, and she wore no makeup. Margaret, in an understated wool dress that ended at her knee and a plain gold necklace, wondered if she had mistakenly overdressed. Rebecca was wearing jeans and a loose green plaid shirt.

"Come in," Rebecca said. The house seemed very quiet: no voices, no background music.

The hall was papered in an expensive, dark wallpaper, fussy with loops and garlands and overblown roses. Several suitcases were stacked at the foot of the flight of carpeted stairs. One of them was open and half-full, as though awaiting the last folded garments.

"Come upstairs," Rebecca said, very subdued as she led the way.

The square, high-ceilinged room was, as Margaret had projected, a riot of country quaintness, with braided rugs and colonial furniture, brass candlesticks, bunches of dried roses in cranberry vases, and a fireplace with aggressive black andirons. A faux American primitive painting hung above the fireplace. There was no butter churn in evidence.

And there were no delicious smells of cooking or coffee, no loaded buffet table, no pitchers of Bloody Marys. There were no people, except for Rebecca, and, after a moment, Peter, who strolled in from a white kitchen festooned with shiny cooper cookware.

"I say," Margaret said, feeling a sudden sense of alarm, "surely I didn't mistake the time."

Neither of her hosts was smiling. Rebecca turned away and picked up a coffee mug resting on a tiny table beside a particularly hideous Staffordshire china dog.

"You're right on time," Peter said. "Let me take your coat."

"The others . . ."

"We cancelled them," Peter said. "Rebecca is leaving to visit her mother."

"Peter thinks I've been doing too much," she said in a small voice. "He thinks I need to get away for a time."

"And I'm flying out to the West Coast," Peter said. "I've had a job offer."

"I see," Margaret said. "You might have called me to cancel. Only yesterday, Rebecca said . . . Well, perhaps I ought to be leaving, then." She hadn't yet surrendered her coat. She'd walk a few blocks to the elevated station, or she'd go to the diner and try to call a taxi.

"Sit down, Lady Margaret," Peter said, and his tone indicated that leaving right now was not an option. "I thought we three ought to have a talk before we left."

"I hope you aren't planning to do something foolish," Margaret said, more bravely than she felt. "I don't think simply leaving town will solve any problems."

"I've done only one—no, two—foolish things in my life," Peter said.

"Frances Rassell?" Margaret asked. "And Sandlot—or should I say Sandy Krofft? I don't know what's worse: murder or having the wrath of Carolyn Sue Hoopes on your head."

"Sandlot." Peter shook his head. "That's effectively finished. Haven't you spoken to your great friend Mrs. Hoopes since Friday?"

"What has Carolyn Sue done?" Margaret asked. She was afraid that the lure of precious stones and fine fabrics had not been enough to amuse her on a Saturday afternoon in New York City.

"Sandy called this morning to say that she'd been fired along with that lout Mascarpone. The Castrocani offices have been taken over by a crew of Mrs. Hoopes's business associates from Dallas. We tried to keep everything about Sandlot out of the files, but—" He gazed at her. "Sandy wasn't entirely clear, but she seems to think you discovered something and told Mrs. Hoopes. I can survive that, but I don't appreciate your interference."

"Carolyn Sue would have eventually figured out on her own that you were making a small fortune acting as the broker for all those real estate transactions for Sandlot. What's to become of all that property?"

Rebecca spoke up bitterly. "Sandy wasn't sure, but she thought there'd be a 'problem' because she used Castrocani money and connections."

"Don't worry, Rebecca," Peter said. "Our money is safe."

Margaret stood up. "Now that you know I helped put Carolyn Sue on the track of Sandlot, I'll be leaving."

"No!" Peter said. "You're going to tell me exactly what else you think you know."

"Ah, Frances. And Tommy Falco." Margaret sat down again. "I only know that Frances was going to expose you, and you killed her. Then Tommy seemed to know something, so he had to die." Margaret suppressed the thought that she knew something, too, and her fate didn't look much rosier than Tommy Falco's. "Frances had a photo of you and Sandy, suggesting an intimacy beyond business."

Peter dismissed the picture with a wave of his hand. "Sandy and I were involved in this Sandlot business, and she was attracted to me. You don't deflect Sandy Krofft easily. I went along, but all I care about is what Rebecca wants and needs."

There was a sudden spark of spirit from Rebecca. "Peter, you keep saying you did it all for me, but you have never had any idea of what it is I want. You run around claiming to be protecting me, but you never listen, and you just loved making all that money." She was nearly pouting. "I worked so hard, and then that awful woman . . ."

"Don't say anything more, sweetheart," Peter said warningly.

Rebecca did not heed him. "That awful, awful Frances Rassell, sneaking around and spying. She was going to ruin my chance of getting the account for the new building. She said she'd tell Sandy. . . . She said she'd tell Peter. . . ." She stopped. "Then she said that she knew what Peter was up to, and she wanted him to come around to her house to talk about it because she was going to tell everyone." Rebecca looked at Margaret, desperate for understanding. "What would my clients think if Peter were involved in a scandal? The Starks and all their friends? Harry Dowd?"

Margaret stood up casually and went to the windows, as though taking time to consider Rebecca's empty questions. She must know already what the Harry Dowds of the world thought of her. There was no one in sight on the street. Margaret gauged the distance to the stairs and her chances of flying down them and out the front door.

"So you arranged to meet Frances at the construction site," Margaret said to Rebecca, "and you killed her. Then you learned that Tommy had spoken to your husband about seeing the murder, and you killed him. Did you set the bomb, too?"

"Of course not! I don't know anything about explosives."

"You have one thing wrong," Peter said, "and please don't try to run down the stairs. You can't get away so easily."

"What do I have wrong?" Margaret asked.

"I did kill Frances," Rebecca said. "I had to."

"And I killed Tommy Falco," Peter said. "He might have said something that would point to Rebecca. We couldn't have that. Right, sweetheart?"

Margaret was highly uncomfortable alone in the dark basement of the Wellingtons' house. One narrow horizontal window near the ceiling provided some dim light, but there was no escape there and no exit except for the stairs up to the ground floor. Peter had closed the door firmly behind him. She had tried it after he left and found it was locked.

Margaret shivered. Peter had taken away her coat and her handbag, and the basement was chilly, although she thought that behind one of the closed and locked doors was a furnace periodically roaring to life. There was a big old-fashioned cast-iron sink with rusty water. She wouldn't die of thirst, but her prospects otherwise were doubtful. She did not know what the Wellingtons had in mind. Would they kill her, too, and blithely fly off to whatever new life they envisioned, leaving behind their quaint little house, the hanging copper ware, and the cashmere afghan, made just for snuggling up in front of the fire on a wintry day . . . ?

She paced back and forth. A couple of straight chairs, a workbench without tools. Cartons piled up in the corners: books and old curtains, business papers and sets of dishes that looked as though they'd been inherited from somebody's grandmother. The single light bulb wasn't working, and the light from outside would fade soon.

At least they hadn't tied her up.

She felt a rush of panic. There was no telling what they'd do to her. True, they were not entirely bereft of human feeling. Peter admitted that he had pretended to Father Steve that someone had come with the message about Tommy, but there had been no messenger. Peter already knew Tommy was dead.

And presumably, Peter loved his wife. Of course, as an example of his devotion, he had whacked Margaret over the head to keep her from approaching Rebecca as she sat in the white car with the dealer.

Stop it, she told herself, and think.

She made another circle of the basement, trying the doors of the closets. All locked.

Carolyn Sue knew where Margaret was going, but if she was engaged in wholesale reorganization of Castrocani Development, it was not likely that she would even think of Margaret until much later.

Would later be too late?

Maybe they intended to leave her here until she dried up and fell into a pile of dust.

She started at a skittering sound at the back of the basement. A gray field mouse appeared from behind the boxes piled up against the back wall and quickly retreated. Margaret walked over to the spot where it had disappeared, and stopped. All old houses had mice, but . . . She bent down. Near the floor she felt a cold draft of air.

There were no sounds from above, although an hour or so earlier, she had heard footsteps above her, as though the Wellingtons were completing packing their luggage. It was after five now, and the light from the sliver of window was fading. Soon she'd be left entirely in the dark.

Carefully she began to move the boxes away from the wall. Some were heavy, and she hoped she wouldn't be forced to unpack cartons of law books to get to the wall. The stream of cold air was stronger now.

On the bottom of the pile was an air conditioner that required great effort to move, but there before her was a door. She almost sobbed when she turned the knob and the door moved slightly. Try as she might, she couldn't budge it further. It seemed to hang crookedly, as though the house had settled over the century and knocked the door out of alignment.

She tried again, this time pulling and lifting up at the same time. The door opened another inch. She rested for a moment and tried again. Another inch. She peered through the crack. There seemed to be a small room or a hallway, almost pitch-black. It might end in a blank wall, or it might show her the way out.

Lady Margaret Priam needed enough space to squeeze through, and she was determined to get it.

The light had almost disappeared from the small window when Margaret finally pulled the door wide enough to fit through. She immediately stumbled over some object on the floor in the dark space where she found herself. She walked carefully, stretching out her arms to gauge the size of the space. It seemed to be a narrow hallway. She could almost touch the walls on either side by reaching out her hands. Blind in the darkness, she moved ahead eight or ten feet and ran into a wall.

Not a wall at all, she discovered with relief, but another door. She fumbled with the knob, and this one opened easily. She found herself confronted by a flimsy grille covering yet another door, this one with a round window that looked out on a dismal garden with masses of tall brown stalks and tangled dead vines on the chain-link fence that separated it from the neighboring garden.

The grille was padlocked closed with a rusty lock. Margaret fought back the rush of despair and saw her freedom. A key hung from a nail beside the door. She managed to unlock the padlock and draw the grille aside. The door to the outside was fastened only with a hook and eye latch.

As she pushed the door to freedom open, she froze. Behind her in the basement, she could hear Peter's voice at the top of the stairs, telling Rebecca to wait where she was.

Now or never, Margaret thought.

As she stepped out into the garden, she heard Peter shout. He was bigger than Margaret, so he couldn't squeeze through the space she'd made without opening the door further, but the delay would not be long.

The chain-link fence was rather more formidable than she had thought, and there was no gate into the next yard. She dragged a rusting metal lawn chair to the fence and managed to climb over, only to tumble to the ground on the other side with a tear in her dress and a twisted ankle.

The house that rose up above the garden she was in was dark, but there were lights showing in the next house. The second fence did have a gate into the next garden. She peered into the French doors that opened onto a flagstone terrace. The room was dark, but there were lights on the floor above.

She looked over her shoulder. Peter had not come into view, but it was only a matter of time. She pounded on the glass. A dog barked inside, and barked again, but no one appeared. Margaret gave up and went on to the next garden. Another fence to scale, but this one was easy, although her ankle was in pain.

Beyond the last fence was a narrow alley lined with trash cans. At the end of it, the street.

She was cold and disheveled, with a rip in her dress, a painful ankle, and a scraped knee that felt damp, as though blood was seeping through her stockings. But she had escaped—without a coat or money, to be sure, but someone would surely spare her a coin to call Manhattan. De Vere or Carolyn Sue or Dianne would send a car.

"You went to a lot of unnecessary trouble," Peter Wellington said. He and Rebecca were standing on the pavement on the end of the alley. "Give her her coat, Rebecca, not her bag. That's right. We'll be three good friends taking an evening stroll."

"Are you absolutely mad?" Margaret said. She felt like crying, but Priams do not cry except when the faithful old dog has to be put down.

"No," Peter said. He looked serious but somehow innocuous in his round glasses and dark chesterfield overcoat with a narrow velvet collar. "I'm saving our skins and buying time."

"Peter, we don't have to do this," Rebecca said tearfully. "We'll explain how it happened, Frances and Tommy Falco. It was all a mistake. She shouldn't have to die, too. . . ."

Whatever Margaret had thought the Wellingtons had in store for her, she had suppressed the idea that they might kill her as well.

"I know what's best, sweetheart," Peter said. He gripped Margaret's arm and, with Rebecca on her other side, walked her along the silent street toward the construction site.

Was no one going to appear? Margaret wondered. Was everyone in Arcadia such a devotee of "Sixty Minutes" that their eyes were locked onto the television screen and they had no time to notice the suspicious trio hurrying along in the night?

"You're hurting me," Margaret said with all the anger she could muster. Peter loosened his grip, and Margaret took her chance. She wasn't prepared to end up dead in the cold dirt of Carolyn Sue's foundation.

She ran. The diner wasn't far away, and that meant safety—unless Spiros was a coconspirator in murder.

It was difficult to run with the pain from her ankle and now her knee, and she could hear Peter closing in on her. The lights of the diner beckoned, but they were still so far.

Margaret gasped and drew on her last bit of strength. She heard a thud behind her, but she didn't stop to look back.

"Lady Margaret!"

She stopped then and turned. Father Steve was standing beside a downed Peter Wellington. Rebecca was coming up the street.

"Father?" Margaret limped back to him.

He grinned. "I wish I could say I played tackle for Notre Dame, but that's not true. I merely tripped him."

Headlights were visible on the street as a car proceeded slowly toward them.

Peter struggled to sit up.

"Mrs. Hoopes became alarmed when you didn't call her, and she couldn't get anyone to answer the Wellingtons' telephone. I'm not quite clear on why she thought there was some difficulty, but she asked me to check on your whereabouts."

The car stopped beside them.

"Any trouble here?"

"De Vere! I . . . I had an invitation to brunch. I didn't tell you."

De Vere got out of the car. "When I got to the apartment tonight, Carolyn Sue was in a fine Texas tizzy about you. Hello, Father Steve. Always something happening in your quiet little parish."

Peter Wellington got to his feet and put his arm around Rebecca.

"I have nothing to say," Peter said, "and neither does my wife."

Chapter 22

"*Never in* my entire life have Ah been so totally *humiliated*," Carolyn Sue said. "To think Ah prided myself on my business sense."

She stood in the middle of Paul's living room surrounded by a vast array of expensive luggage. She was already wearing her huge dark glasses, prepared to step out of New York into the tropical sun. Her cream-colored linen pants and jacket made a nice contrast to the tan that had not faded during her few hectic days in the north.

Margaret nodded sympathetically. "I'm sure your people will straighten these business things out. The police will handle everything else, now that Casey and Arthur have come out of hiding. Spiros has not exactly denied that he was receiving a tidy sum from Johnny to keep the neighborhood on edge with aggressive acts. Just our bad luck that one of his minions discovered how to make a bomb out of olive oil and worry beads."

"What! Oh, you're joshin me," Carolyn Sue said. "His boys picked up a bit of dynamite or something. Mr. Spiros is quite an interestin' man. Very European. But don't I know how playin' around with real estate can drive a person to all kinds of mischief. It's kind of like playing Monopoly for real—today Boardwalk and Park Place, tomorrow the entire borough of Queens." Carolyn Sue fussed around with an errant curl. "Are you sure you and De Vere want to drive me to the airport? My hired limo would suit me fine."

"I know it's not as elegant," Margaret said, "but I promised Paul that I would personally see you to the first-class lounge. Besides, I want to give Sam a taste of the excitement of being on the brink of a long, lovely trip somewhere."

"You sure did earn your money," Carolyn Sue said. "What's to become of those poor Wellington folks?"

"I suggest a plea of madness for the one and an overpowering desire to protect the sacred family unit for the other."

Carolyn Sue sniffed. "The things people get away with nowadays. Murder is murder where I come from, and you don't go free." She paused to reconsider. "Unless, of course, you get yourself one of those simple country lawyers. A good ol' boy with a big hat, shiny boots, and a devious legal mind that won't quit . . . Here's Sam now. Sam, honey, y'all should be traveling south with me. Ben would love havin' you."

De Vere looked at Margaret. "I'm considering it," he said. "It may be the only way to keep Margaret away from murder—cast her away on a remote tropical island."

About the Author

JOYCE CHRISTMAS has written seven previous novels: *Hidden Assets* (with Jon Peterson), *Blood Child*, *Dark Tide*, *Suddenly in Her Sorbet*, *Simply to Die For*, *A Fête Worse Than Death*, *A Stunning Way to Die*, and *Friend or Faux*. In addition, she has spent a number of years as a book and magazine editor. She lives in New York City.

MORE MURDER AND MAYHEM

from
Joyce Christmas